MW01251273

Everyone's Child

Cathy McGough

Stratford Living Publishing

WHAT READERS ARE SAYING...

FROM THE US:
"Cathy McGough's Everyone's Child is a psychological thriller that will have you wondering right to the astonishing end."

"Wow, I most definitely wasn't expecting and couldn't have predicted the ending to this story."

"A well constructed, plot-driven story."

"There were so many twists and turns and just when you had it all figured out, the rug was yanked out from underneath you."

"I was stunned midway through the book, which had me really thinking WTH?"

FROM THE UK:
"A story that is so tightly written that packs a punch."

"I thought I had it all worked out, but I was so wrong."

"An enjoyable read with some surprising twists along the way."

FROM CA:
"I found the storyline was intriguing and enjoyed reading the book to the end."

"Easy to read, fast paced, and has an interesting premise."

FROM IN:
"A well written enjoyable thriller."

CONTENTS

DEDICATION   XI

Poem   XIII

1. CHAPTER ONE   1

2. CHAPTER TWO   5

3. CHAPTER THREE   7

4. CHAPTER FOUR   10

5. CHAPTER FIVE   11

6. CHAPTER SIX   14

7. CHAPTER SEVEN   16

8. CHAPTER EIGHT   17

9. CHAPTER NINE   19

10. CHAPTER TEN   20

11. CHAPTER ELEVEN   29

12. CHAPTER TWELVE   34

13. ***   37

14. CHAPTER THIRTEEN   39

15. ***   44

16. CHAPTER FOURTEEN   48

17. CHAPTER FIFTEEN   50

18. ***   51

19. ***   54

20. ***   56

21. CHAPTER SIXTEEN   58

22. CHAPTER SEVENTEEN   60

23. CHAPTER EIGHTEEN   61

24. CHAPTER NINETEEN   64

25. CHAPTER TWENTY   66

26. CHAPTER TWENTY-ONE   69

27. ***   71

28. CHAPTER TWENTY-TWO   74

29. ***   76

30. CHAPTER TWENTY-THREE   79

31. ***   81

32. ***   82

33. CHAPTER TWENTY-FOUR   88

34. CHAPTER TWENTY-FIVE   90

35. CHAPTER TWENTY-SIX   93

36. CHAPTER TWENTY-SEVEN   98

37. CHAPTER TWENTY-EIGHT   100

38. CHAPTER TWENTY-NINE   102

39. CHAPTER THIRTY   104

40. CHAPTER THIRTY-ONE   109

41. ***   112

42. CHAPTER THIRTY-TWO   115

43. CHAPTER THIRTY-THREE   119

44. ***   124

45. ***   127

46. CHAPTER THIRTY-FOUR   128

47. CHPTER THIRTY-FIVE   130

48. CHAPTER THIRTY-SIX   132

49. CHAPTER THIRTY-SEVEN   135

50. CHAPTER THIRTY-EIGHT   137

51. CHAPTER THIRTY-NINE   139

52. ***   143

53. ***   145

54. ***   146

55. CHAPTER FORTY   148

56. CHAPTER FORTY-ONE   151

57. ***   155

58. CHAPTER FORTY-TWO   157

59. CHAPTER FORTY-THREE   159

60. CHAPTER FORTY-FOUR   160

61. CHAPTER FORTY-FIVE   161

62. CHAPTER FORTY-SIX   163

63. CHAPTER FORTY-SEVEN   165

64. CHAPTER FORTY-EIGHT   166

65. CHAPTER FORTY-NINE   168

66. CHAPTER FIFTY   169

67. CHAPTER FIFTY-ONE   171

68. CHAPTER FIFTY-TWO   172

69. CHAPTER FIFTY-THREE   173

70. CHAPTER FIFTY-FOUR   175

71. CHAPTER FIFTY-FIVE   177

72. CHAPTER FIFTY-SIX   180

73. CHAPTER FIFTY-SEVEN   182

74. CHAPTER FIFTY-EIGHT   183

75. CHAPTER FIFTY-NINE   184

76. CHAPTER SIXTY   186

77. CHAPTER SIXTY-ONE   188

78. CHAPTER SIXTY-TWO   189

79. CHAPTER SIXTY-THREE   191

80. CHAPTER SIXTY-FOUR   192

81. CHAPTER SIXTY-FIVE   195

82. CHAPTER SIXTY-SIX   198

83. CHAPTER SIXTY-SEVEN   200

84. CHAPTER SIXTY-EIGHT   202

85. EPILOGUE   207

Acknowledgments   209

About The Author   211

Also by: 213

For The Children.

POEM

THE PAPER DOLL

The paper doll is tangled in the
whirl of the wind

Drained of emotion she twirls and
she spins

Around and around, ballerina-like
pirouettes

Flashing back to life's failures and
regrets.

Frantically trying from its clutches
to escape

In her ears the wind is whispering
rape.

The paper doll is torn from limb to
limb

A mere memory of what could
have been.

She feels no pain for she is only a
child

She feels nothing.

Hear the cry of the children as they
toss and turn

In the dreams of their sleep

Protect them from the whirlwinds
of life.

Run, children run,

There are no chains to bind you
any longer.

Protect them from the whirlwinds
of life.

CHAPTER ONE

BENJAMIN

Seventeen-year-old Benjamin was a conscientious employee. Especially since he dropped out of high school. Twice a day, six days a week he visited the bank. In the morning, for cash. In the afternoon to deposit the day's takings. Walking there and back was uneventful: until this particular morning.

What caught his eye, was a woman. Strutting in high high heels, she stood out like a mannequin on a beach. The gold tags on her handbag and sunglasses reflected the light, causing it to bounce and move about like fireflies. Over the shoulder of her sleeveless black dress trailed a red scarf.

Benjamin's eyes followed the flow of the scarf, until it reached the end of the woman's outstretched arm. Attached to it was a little girl who was struggling to keep up. The child, perhaps seven years old's arm also reached back. Attached to it was a thing: a gangly life-size doll. He did a double take because the doll's face and the child's face were carbon copies. Then he noticed the doll's outstretched arm also reached back - to nothing and no one. The thing's gangly legs and shoes scuffed along the pavement bringing up the rear.

Curious, he followed the strange trio as they turned the corner en route to Lake Ontario's Waterfront promenade.

The woman stopped, yanked the reluctant follower's arm, then picked up the pace. The little one stumbled to the ground without letting go of her doll's hand. She scrambled to her feet only to receive a backhanded slap on the cheek. A slap, the sound of which caused him to cringe as it seemed to reverberate.

The woman walked rapidly as the child's peep turned into a shriek. She leaned back, whispering into the child's ear: result silent tears.

Placing his finger on speed dial 911, he assessed the situation. If he were a full-grown man – he'd give her the what for. Instead, he continued shadowing them. Watching. Pacing himself wondering what the big hurry was.

The doll bouncing along behind with a toothy grin gave him the creeps, so he crossed over to the other side of the road. He continued observing the strange trio. In specific how the woman's red scarf contrasted with her raven black hair and dress. She seemed out of place, like she was on the way to a magazine shoot with two kids in tow.

Wait a minute. The type of doll seemed familiar. His boss, Abe, sometimes ordered similar dolls through his shop. Usually in the months leading up to Christmas.

The dolls were designed and shipped from Europe. Each order required a photo of the child. This was to replicate complexion, hair, and eye colour. Details like height, weight and shoe size were recorded on the back of the photo.

It was then he noticed why the little girl was struggling. On her feet she wore sparkly sandals, the kind with the wrap around ankle band. As sandals went, they were pretty, but unsuitable for fast paced walking. For her twin, the sandals weren't a problem as the doll was pulled along the sidewalk.

By the time they arrived at the first park bench, the woman had calmed down. She laughed when she helped the little one to remove her backpack. Then ensured she was comfortably seated before attending to the doll. She bent its legs and propped it up in a seated position.

He moved closer, taking photos of the waterfront until his phone vibrated. It was Abe, checking up on him.

"Where are you?" Abe had texted. Abe was Benjamin's boss and landlord. Abe was a stickler for routines.

"Lineup, B back ASAP," the boy texted.

Abe's reply was a thumb's up emoji.

The woman kneeled, so she was eye to eye with the child.

The teenager took a full panoramic shot of the Lake Ontario skyline from the CN Tower to Burlington.

"Darling, I forgot my wallet," she patted the child's hand. "I'll be right back, I promise."

The child remained quiet, fiddling with her sandals.

"Do your feet hurt, darling? I'm sorry we had to rush. You can rest here, and you'll be fine by the time I come back to collect you. Just wait here, okay?"

The child nodded and dropped her legs down. Unable to touch the ground, she kept still.

"While I'm gone, don't move from this bench." She glanced around. "And don't talk to anyone. Remember, we have a secret word. Know what it is? Shh, don't tell me. You recall it, yes?"

"What if I have to," the child whispered, "pee?"

"Hold it until I get back. I won't be long. The sooner I go, the sooner I'll return." She stood and straightened her back.

The little one grabbed her arm, "You won't forget me, will you Mommy? Like last time?"

The woman sighed and whispered.

"Darling." She patted her daughter's hand. "I collected you from school on time ninety-nine times and you always remember that one time I was late." She took a deep breath, then stepped back.

"Sorry, Mommy."

The teenager sat on a bench nearby, scrolling through the photos he'd taken. He glanced up, as the woman turned. Her facial expression seemed more childlike now, with her chin thrust forward.

3

"This time I know the way home," her daughter said with a smirk.

The woman huffed, turned back, and hugged her daughter. "I've got to go now, baby."

"I'm not a baby."

"I know you're not. Wait here, wait for me. I'll be back. Cross my heart." She mimed the heart crossing then walked away.

"See you soon, Mommy," the child said. She craned her neck, watching the gap grow between herself and her mother.

The teenager looked on with tear-filled eyes. She was a good mother after all, or better than he thought she was.

The mother turned around and blew her little girl a kiss, then continued walking.

His phone vibrated again. Abe. He had to get to the bank.

The child unzipped her backpack, pulled out a book and began reading. For a minute or two, he watched her. It was cute, how she moved her lips to sound out the words.

He checked his watch. More certain now her mother would return as promised, he went to the bank.

It was the only way to stop Abe from coming to look for him. If Abe had to come out of the store to search for him...

He didn't want to think about it.

CHAPTER TWO

JENNIFER WALKER

When she was a few feet away, Jennifer, glanced back at her daughter who remained as instructed on the bench. She hated to leave her alone there, but what choice did she have after what she'd done? She opened her phone camera and snapped a photo of her daughter. The photo showed her little girl framed by the bluest sky and the even bluer water of Lake Ontario. Content her daughter wouldn't budge, she turned in the direction from which they'd come.

As she made her way back, she thought about her partner Mark Wheeler. She'd been going out with him for a while, even though she knew he was already married.

For the most part, at least when they were out in public or when her daughter was around, he was kind and gentle.

But there was a different side to him when they were alone with sex on the menu. True, sometimes she enjoyed bondage, even a little erotic spanking. However, the erotic asphyxiation took things too far. The feeling of going under the water, down, down, down. Gasping for breath like you'd never find it again was one which frightened her. So, this time she put her foot down and refused to do it. Mark went ahead and did it to himself while she went to take a shower. When she returned, he was dead. She'd been too frightened to even remove the plastic bag from his head. Instead, she went to her daughter's room and spent the night there and first thing in the morning, they left the house.

Her phone rang, it was him at last. "You have to help me," she said. "I've nowhere else to turn."

"Is it Mark?" her friend, also Mark's driver Poncho asked.

She sobbed. "Yes."

"Okay, I'll be right there. I'm about fifteen minutes away. Hang tough."

To distract herself a memory of Katie as a newborn popped into her mind as she relived the first time that she held her. Her daughter was the tiniest, softest, most beautiful little angel she'd ever seen. She was growing up so fast. Jennifer hated leaving her daughter alone at the waterfront, but they had to get rid of the body. Especially with Mark's connection to the community, and to the drug world. Even if she told them the truth, they'd never believe her. Mark's father had bags of money – and she couldn't risk going to prison. What would happen to her baby?

She laughed, thinking about how many times she accused her mother of doing daft things for men who weren't worth it. She looked up at the sky, "Mom, I'm sorry as this thing I did takes the prize." History always repeated itself. Knowing this didn't make her feel any better.

Stop beating yourself up, you silly fool, she thought. She'd be going back for Katie before she knew it. Besides, in her backpack her daughter had a book. The doll which they called Katie Jr. while her daughter tried to figure out what to name it, gave her the creeps. He'd given it to her. She'd get her another doll and toss that one into the bin.

Almost home now, Jennifer spotted a white van waiting in the driveway. Poncho pulled the car inside the garage, then she closed it. She entered through the front door and let Poncho in hoping her nosy neighbour across the street was otherwise occupied.

CHAPTER THREE

KATIE

After reading the book to her doll twice, Katie put it away. She watched the seagulls as they flew up, then down so fast pushing their beaks into the water. Sometimes they'd pop back up carrying a small fish in their beaks. She applauded when this happened. More than once, people passing by stopped to see what she was clapping at and joined in with her. Katie felt less alone when this happened.

"She's so cute," a young couple said to her. As they were strangers, she said nothing, but continued watching the seagulls.

Time went by, as the sun moved down the sky little by little and a policeman stopped. "Is everything okay?"

'Don't talk to strangers,' her mother's voice said in her head. He was a policeman though. He was someone you could trust in times of trouble. "I'm waiting for my mommy. She'll be back in a minute."

The policeman must've believed her, as he tipped his hat and walked on.

"Thank you," she said, hoping to see her mother walking toward her. She closed her eyes and opened them again, hoping for a different result. No such luck.

Katie flattened her red dress on the front. She lifted the sleeve a little where the elastic was pinching her and leaving a mark. She rocked forwards and back. The mere movement caused the ankle part of her sandals to tighten up, so she ceased moving her legs.

Last night Mark and Mommy had tucked her into bed. Then she heard noises. When they were loud – yelled – it was scary, but not scary enough to keep her from falling asleep.

Her mommy always said, "Katie, you could sleep through a tornado." This made her laugh.

When they left the house this morning, mommy said Mark was sleeping in. That's why they needed to get dressed and out of the house in a hurry.

When the curtains moved across the street Katie said, "She's looking again, Mommy."

"Don't worry about that nosy old bat," her mother said, pulling her daughter along with the doll bringing up the rear.

Mark wasn't Katie's real father, but he came over a lot. He sometimes bought her things, like her doll. When he was around, her mother was happy, at first. Then he'd go away, and her mother would say he was never coming back. But he always did.

The little girl lived in a constant state of confusion. Men came and went. Still, she loved the doll which was her twin.

Problem was, what to name her. She couldn't call her Katie Two because twins don't have the same first name. Even though she'd had her for a while the doll still remained nameless.

The child didn't miss having a father most of the time. Children don't often miss something they never had. Until society reminds them – such as a Father's Day Luncheon at school.

"Will you be my daddy, at school for the Father's Day Luncheon?" Katie asked Mark.

"I'd love to darling," he replied.

"But Mark is a busy man," her mother said.

When Father's Day arrived, Katie was the only child there without someone. Other children without fathers, brought grandfathers, brothers, or uncles. Katie, who didn't have any of those either, was even more distraught.

When Katie burst into tears at the dinner table, her mother called the Principal. She demanded the school ban Father's Day events altogether.

Katie didn't want it canceled for everyone. All she wanted was inclusion. Mark being there would have made everything okay for everyone.

A seagull swooped nearby. The bird pooped mid-flap, leaving a souvenir behind. It splattered over the child's and the doll's dresses. Katie wiped the tears away from her eyes first. Then she did the same for the doll.

She wished her mother would hurry on back.

CHAPTER FOUR

BENJAMIN

Now late afternoon and Benjamin was heading to the bank. He glanced in the direction of the waterfront: the child was still there! He'd been right in his initial gut feeling - her mother was a disgraceful parent. Leaving a little girl all alone at the waterfront all day was abandonment.

He hurried on to the bank. He had to get rid of the day's takings before the bank closed. Instead of risking waiting, he deposited the cash into the machine, then returned to check on the little girl.

Abe had already texted him twice asking where r u?

At first, he had thought it was exciting to introduce Abe to technology, but now, it was a pain in the ass. Not that Abe distrusted Benjamin. In fact, the man and his wife were Benjamin's legal guardians. Although Abe was in the people business, selling goods to the public, he was not a people person.

"Need 2 t/c of something 1st," the teenager replied.

"Okie, dokie," Abe replied. "Must call the wife out of the kitchen to help!"

He chuckled before sending an appropriate emoji as he made his way back to check on the little girl.

CHAPTER FIVE

KATIE

Katie remained on the park bench. On the horizon she could see the sun was coming down. It was getting late. Her mother had forgotten her–again. The child had to urinate and considered walking home. She knew the way but didn't have a key. She wished she'd worn her runners, or less pinchy sandals.

She didn't want to be outside when it went dark. Even now she imagined shadows forming around her, made by cloud reflections. When a crow cawed, she jumped and shivered. A ladybug crawled up her leg, onto her dress. She lifted it to her finger and let it walk up her arm, until it left a yellow streak as it walked.

"It's okay," she whispered to the insect, "everybody pees." She deposited the pretty red bug onto the bench and off it flew.

Her stomach rumbled and she fumbled in her bag and pulled out a melted mini-Kit-Kat. It tasted so good, but she sure wished it wasn't a mini and hoped her mother would be back soon.

The child pretended to feed the doll, then went back to reading.

She'd read the book so many times that her mind drifted back to earlier in the day when her mother told her she wouldn't be going to school today.

"Why?" she asked. "I want to go to school."

"Today we're going to go to the waterfront. We'll watch the birds, listen to the waves, and later we'll go to the café for baby chinos."

"I'm not a baby anymore," Katie protested.

"I know you're not, but don't you still love Baby Chinos?"

The little girl thrust her chin out, thinking about Baby Chinos. She was a big girl now, and when her mommy came to collect her, she'd order an extra-large strawberry milkshake instead.

"It will be such fun!" her mother's voice echoed in her ears.

"Such fun," the child repeated. Then her mind wandered, "Can I bring her?" Katie had asked. This was in reference to her doll.

"Yes, you can, as long as you carry her all the way there and all the way back. And remember, you'll have your backpack on too."

"Okay Mommy, I will." Katie put her arms through the backpack straps and wrapped her arms around the waist of the doll.

Above her, a V-shaped group of Canadian Geese honked their way across the sky. She noticed the sun had gone down a little bit more. She shivered and took the doll's hand into hers as footsteps neared. They belonged to a person who when she saw him, she realized he wasn't a boy or a man– he was somewhere in between.

She folded her arms around herself. As the sun sunk further down, and she wished she had a sweater or a coat. She observed the boy/man wore neither. His black t-shirt had a rock on the front, and under it the words, ZOOM! reminded her of the television show with the same name. The boy/man had a golden tan on his face and arms. He wore black jeans and runners.

Darkness was coming and she wanted her mother to return and take her home again. Until then, she wished that the boy/man would say something, anything to her.

Even though she wasn't supposed to speak to strangers, the sound of someone else's voice when she felt like this would comfort her. Although, the boy/man more than likely had been told the same thing – don't talk to strangers.

The other thing was, if he did speak to her, she'd probably cry. She didn't want him to think she was a baby, because if he did, he'd call a policeman and he'd find out that this wasn't the first time her mother had forgotten to collect her.

She picked up her book and used it as a wall so the boy/man wouldn't see her falling tears.

CHAPTER SIX

BENJAMIN

He walked by, to see if she'd speak to him, she hadn't said a word, but she looked so sad, then she hid behind her book. He kept on walking, then hid in the bushes behind her so he could keep an eye on her without her knowing.

Once, he remembered, when he and the other children were playing outside, a man had gone by. He stopped and spoke to one of the girls, then returned in his car and tried to coax her inside. Benjamin ran and told their foster parents what happened. He even memorized the license plate number which allowed them to report it to the police.

It was one of the few times they'd listened to him and he and the other children were banned from playing in the front yard.

This little girl was in a terrible situation and soon it would get worse when it was fully dark. Yes, there was a streetlamp near the bench, but it was making her more vulnerable. She was as conspicuous as a lighthouse in a storm.

He brushed his hand against the evergreen bush. The sweet smell of Christmas brought back memories of times gone by. Like the first Christmas at the home of Abe and El. They'd given him more presents than he'd received in all his Christmases added together.

He shook his head, wondering if he should call the police? No, he'd wait a little longer. He wanted to be wrong. He wanted her mother to come back and fetch her. He decided to give her a little more time.

He parted the branches, their scratchy needles made him itch.

Benjamin's mother and father would never have left him alone like this. Not on purpose. They died when he was a boy, made him an orphan – through no fault of their own. Accidents happened, yes, he knew about accidents. An accident would explain everything.

The little girl was cold and and she shivered as the sun dropped lower and lower on the horizon.

Having no coat to offer her, all he had to offer was a friendly face, but first he needed to think up a Plan A. And when he had that firmly placed in his mind, he needed a Plan B.

She squatted behind the bushes to think.

CHAPTER SEVEN

KATIE

Whoosh, whoosh, she heard as the wind tickled the trees as day turned to night. She heard noises behind her, but she was afraid to turn around. Instead, she grabbed the doll's other hand and held both of them against her chest.

She remembered a time when her mother decided to teach her a lesson. They'd been in the movie theatre. She said she would buy more popcorn.

"Don't speak to anyone and don't turn around."

"Okay, Mommy."

From the back row, what Katie didn't know was her mother was watching her. She and another man, not Mark, waited until she turned around.

"Ha!" her mother scolded.

"Ah, leave her alone," her mother's date had said when Katie burst into tears.

Later he left the theatre and they had to take a taxi home.

Katie's mother promised, never to play the game again. She wrapped her arms around herself.

CHAPTER EIGHT

BENJAMIN

After he worked out Plan A and B in his mind, he thought about what he would say. "Everything is going to be okay," he whispered to himself. No, it sounded corny. "I'll take you to somewhere safe," he whispered, would it frighten her? After all he was a stranger. It was a sticky situation, and he didn't want to say the wrong thing.

At the same time, he had to think about his own safety too. He was a teenager, out late, in a public park. Watching a little girl – making sure no harm came to her. To others, his presence might be misconstrued.

Not to mention, boys alone in public spaces could get into all kinds of situations. Especially if packs

of boys came along and wanted to jump him or cause a fight.

Once, a long time ago he'd been pursued relentlessly by such a mob – only getting away because he ran faster. Just thinking about it now brought back all the terrors. He wrapped his arms around himself.

He set a time limit. 'If no one comes to collect her in thirty more minutes,' he whispered, 'then I will speak with her.'

When thirty minutes came and went, he reviewed the plans. Plan A, he would offer to help by walking her home. Plan B, if she didn't know her address, he'd offer to take her to the police station. Either way he wasn't leaving the waterfront until this poor little abandoned child was somewhere, safe.

CHAPTER NINE

KATIE

She sat straight up, alerted by footsteps in the distance. High heels. Her heart swelled. Her mother was coming back to collect her at last!

She lifted the doll, and looked up at the streetlight above her. She imagined the light was streaming down and warming her up. She wished she'd thought of it before, as she wasn't cold anymore. Imagination was a magical thing; you could always think bad things away.

She remembered the other times when her mother had left her. One time she'd been the only child remaining at school at the end of the day. One of the teacher's noticed and took her in to see the Principal like she herself had done something wrong. She hadn't.

Later, when her mother came to collect her the Principal huffed.

On other occasions, her mother had left her for extended periods of time with people she knew. This time was different. She was all alone.

The high heels clicked nearer.

CHAPTER TEN

BENJAMIN AND KATIE

Benjamin rustled in the evergreen shrub, observing the little girl. To him, she was like a little sister, even though they had not previously met. He was wise beyond his age. In the foster system he had to protect others. Once or twice, he had to put himself at risk because no one would listen. Glancing at his phone, he took a deep breath. The second thirty-minute period was over. Then he would go to her.

Heels clicked on the pavement.

He poked his head out of the bushes, waving a branch away. He wanted to see the long-awaited happy reunion. This woman was not the mother. She kept on walking.

He sighed.

Until the woman turned back, and approached the little girl on the bench. She leaned down and whispered something.

"I'm sorry, but I'm not allowed to talk to strangers," Katie said, leaning back.

The woman smelled like she'd taken a bath in the stinky red wine Mommy and Mark drank in fancy glasses. She used her fingers to plug her nose.

"My name is Jenny," she said. "What's your name?"

She did not speak, instead continued to hold her nose to ward off the smell.

"You are too young to be out here all alone. Where are your parents?" The woman looked around and whispered, "Come on and tell me your name, then we won't be strangers anymore."

Benjamin couldn't hear a thing, until the woman said, "Get up!"

And in a flash, he was there, like a grenade had been dropped.

The woman named Jenny reached out her hand and tried to force Katie to take it, but she was still firmly holding her nose with one hand and onto her doll with the other.

"There you are!" he said, wagging his index finger at her. "I told you to count to ten, and then come and find me!"

"I," she said, "I'm sorry."

"Tut," the woman named Jenny said, as she fiddled in her handbag and pulled out her phone. She put it to her ear, began talking and walked away. In the darkness, the sound of her shoes clicking echoed.

"Mind if I wait here with you?" he asked. She nodded and he sat down on the bench beside her. When the sound of heels clicking could no longer be heard he said, "PU, I know now why you were holding your nose!"

"The smell is bad, but it tastes even worse."

"You've tasted wine?" he asked.

"Once, it's a secret. Mommy doesn't know."

"Your secret is safe with me," he said. "Um, would you like me to walk you home?"

"I'm waiting for my mommy. She should come to collect me soon." Her voice wavered and she looked at her feet.

"Is there anyone I can call to collect you? Anyone at all?"

"No. Mommy always comes."

"You don't mind if I wait here with you then?"

"Suit yourself," Katie said.

The trio sat together on the park bench. A blond-haired little girl with a lookalike doll and a dark-haired teenager.

"What's your name?" she asked. "My name is Katie."

"I'm Benjamin, but you can call me Benji, if you like."

"I saw a movie once with a little dog named Benji. He looked scruffy, like you."

He finger-brushed his hair.

"Oh, I didn't mean to," she said. "I mean, you don't look too scruffy."

He laughed and she did too. For a while they listened to the waves slapping upon the rocks and watched the stars dancing in the sky above them.

She shivered.

"Oh, you're cold. I wish I had a coat to give you."

"No matter, it's the thought that counts."

"You're right, it is the thought. but it's also the actions and intentions behind the thoughts which inspired them. What I mean is, the follow through. Do you understand what I'm getting at?" She nodded.

They sat together quietly for a few moments before Benjamin spoke again.

"Did you know you can think the opposite of how you feel, and change everything?"

"I know imagination is power," she said with a raised eyebrow. "But how?"

"Ah, you're a skeptic?"

"Am I?" she hesitated. "What am I?"

"A skeptic is a person who doesn't believe what she's heard – unless she has proof. Would you like me to show you how, to change everything?"

She grinned, "Yes, please!"

He began, "When I'm cold, I sing a song in my head which is opposite to being cold..."

"You mean warm?"

He nodded.

"I don't know any warm songs."

"If you don't know a warm song, you make one up like this:

It's ridiculously hot out today,
My ice cream is melting.
As the sun shines down
As the sun shines down on me.
The chocolate when melting.

Tastes even better

With the sun shining down

With the sun shining down so warmly."

"I know the tune, but it has different words," she said.

"Ah, you recognized I was singing my words to Frère Jacques."

"That's very clever," she said.

"Are you feeling warmer now?"

She'd stopped shivering and the goosebumps on her arms had vanished. "It works!"

They continued to sing the song together, to the tune of Frère Jacques. Soon singing about food, made them both feel hungry.

"Can you whistle?" he asked.

She looked at her feet. "No, but I don't need to know how – not if I know the words."

"True," he said.

They went back to looking up at the sky. When she found the man in the moon, she pretended she was

breaking off a piece of cheese from his face. She offered a bite first to Benji.

"This is the best cheese I've ever tasted."

She took another bite, "I'm so full," she exclaimed with a sigh."

They were quiet for a little while.

"How far away do you live?"

"It's not far, but with these sandals on – they pinch – it would seem like it. Plus, I don't have a key."

"Oh, yes I see your ankles do look red."

"Besides, my mommy told me not to move from this spot."

He crossed his arms. "Okay, we'll wait, but it isn't safe for us, to stay here much longer."

"What about your mom and dad?" she asked, now beginning to feel the cold again and singing the sunny song in her head.

"They are in heaven."

"I'm sorry," she said, patting his hand.

"It's okay, it happened years ago." He was quiet, singing the sunny song in his head. "I have an idea. You could come to my place. You could sleep in the bed and I'll sleep in the big comfy chair. We could come back in the morning, wait for your mother then."

"When my mommy returns, if I've moved an inch – she'll be cross."

"I'll explain everything. She would want you somewhere safe. You will be safe with me."

"Oh," she said, glancing around. "It is dark."

"Yes, and when it's late and dark – well, you can be in the wrong place at the wrong time. Terrible things can happen."

She crossed her arms, now feeling cold again.

"I don't mean to scare you, but I think I should take you home. Maybe your mommy is already there waiting."

"I don't think so, but..."

"It's worth a try," he stood. "Let's see what your doll thinks." He took a few steps, and leaned in, like the doll was whispering into his ear. "Oh yes," he said. "I know, but surely your friend's mommy would understand. Hmm. Yes."

"What's she saying?"

"She wants to go home, too. It's been an awfully long day." Then to the doll, "But Katie's feet are really hurting, we'd have to leave you here so I could piggy-back her home."

"We can't leave her here. She's my best friend."

"And a good friend she is, keeping you company here all day."

He looked at his phone, the battery would run out soon. He couldn't carry her and the doll on his back. Should he hit 911 and get the police to come and collect her? Walking to the police station was an option but it was quite a hike away.

"Do you know the way, to your house?"

"I think so."

"Okay, Katie, so I am suggesting Plan A."

"What is, Plan A?"

"Plan A is, I piggyback you home, so you don't have to walk and hurt your feet even more. If your mommy is home, then I'll come back and bring your doll to you. Does it sound okay with you?"

"Yes, I like Plan A."

"Now Plan B," he said. "If you have a Plan A, you should always have a Plan B too."

She uncrossed her arms and nodded.

"Plan B, only if your mommy isn't home could go one way or another way."

"Which way will I like the best?" she asked, then waited for him to answer.

He reconsidered the options. Should he call the police, or take her home and come back in the morning? He explained.

"Either way, I have to leave my doll here, right?"

"How about we hide her over there in the evergreen shrub? It'll be like she's waiting for you under the Christmas tree! Then, we can come back in the morning and collect her. She'll smell like Christmas and she can tell you all about her adventure."

She leaned over and the doll whispered something. "Okay," she said.

One part of him hoped her mother would be home. The other worried about leaving her with a

mother who didn't bother to collect her. He heard El's voice in his head. 'Don't judge,' she'd say. As always, El – he hoped - would be proven right.

El was married to Abe. They were his legal guardians, his landlords and his employers. Since he dropped out of high school, he spent most of his time with them and knew they'd understand – and want to help.

Benjamin swept his arm down and bowed to her. "My lady, are you ready to be transported home?"

"I forgot something," she said, with her lip in a pout.

His eyebrows arched, "What did you forget?"

"I'm not supposed to talk to strangers."

"Yes, well, we are no longer strangers. You know my name and I know your name, and I'm thrilled to offer you transportation back to your humble home." He went down on one knee.

"Arise!" she commanded, giggling, as she stood upon the bench. Benji turned around, and she threw her arms around his neck and soon they were off.

"Wait a minute," she commanded, pointing to the doll.

"Oops," Benji said, picking up the doll. He hid it under the evergreen bushes.

"You're right," Katie said. "It does smell like Christmas here."

"All set to go now?"

After she told him what it was, Benjamin typed Katie's address into his phone.

She giggled. "Mind if I ask you a question?"

"No, go for it."

"It's personal, about your mommy and daddy."

"I don't mind, it happened a long time ago. Ask away."

"Mommy always tells me I shouldn't get too personal."

"I'm fine with it."

"Do you, talk to them?"

He was surprised. No one ever asked him that question. "No," he replied.

"Never, ever?"

"Nope."

"Turn again here." He turned. "Don't you think they're lonely without you?"

"I," he didn't know how to answer so he didn't for a few minutes. "They left me, alone. It was an accident, but..."

"You don't talk to them because you think the accident was their fault?" She held on more tightly, resting her head against his shoulder.

"I'm not mad at them. They didn't leave me on purpose, but yes, I am mad."

"At god?"

"I was mad at everyone, then I met the Julius.' They took me in and gave me a home. They helped me to build a new life. To be a part of a family again. They even said it was okay to cry. As a boy, I wasn't used to it being okay. You're a little girl, so I shouldn't lay my problems on you. I think we should talk about something else."

The little angel didn't say anything for a few minutes. She was sound asleep.

He soon found out that she was right about the distance. It hadn't been too far at all.

The first thing he noticed straightaway was that her house was in total darkness. He had hoped at least to see the porch light on to welcome the child home. Instead, it too was pitch black and he found it difficult to find the doorbell. He rang it a few times but there was as he'd expected no answer.

He stepped back and ran his eyes over all the surrounding houses along both sides of the street. They too were all engulfed in darkness, although for a second he thought he saw a curtain move on the top floor in the house across the street. Having no other choice, he went back the way he came.

Little Katie wasn't heavy, but she'd get heavier as time passed and to get to his place, it was still a long walk. He was super happy he hadn't agreed to lug along the doll though. He hoped it would be safe enough where it was.

She raised her head, "Did you notice?"

"What?"

"Sometimes the curtain moves across the street. Mommy says we have a nosy neighbour."

"Oh, I didn't notice anything. Are they nice neighbours though?"

"I don't know. Mommy always tells me not to talk to strangers."

"Even your neighbours?"

"Yes, especially our nosy neighbours."

"Okay, Katie, so I think we're on Plan B now."

She yawned. "Plan B."

"Yes, m'lady," he said, picking up the pace. She snored on his shoulder, as a siren went off. He closed his eyes when dust and bits of paper were whipped up by the wind. A dog barked in the distance.

She raised her head as they arrived at the Julius' front door. "We're here," he said, "But shhh, El and Abe are sleeping. My apartment is just up there." He pointed up the stairs. As they reached the top, she snored loudly. He removed her pinchy sandals, then tucked her into bed.

She was half asleep, "I have to pee," she said.

He showed her where the bathroom was then went into the kitchenette where he prepared them toasty cheese sandwiches and hot cocoa.

"Where are you, Benji?" she asked when she came out of the bathroom.

"Right here," Benjamin said, carrying the sandwiches and cocoa on a tray.

After eating, Katie yawned the biggest widest yawn, and settled in to go to sleep. He tucked her in and noticed she was already sound asleep.

He pulled off his shoes and socks and threw a blanket over himself on the comfy chair. He too was asleep in no time at all.

CHAPTER ELEVEN

BENJAMIN AND ABE

In the morning when the first glimpse of light peeked its way in through the curtains, Benjamin woke up. He stretched and for a minute forgot why he was sleeping on the comfy chair. The blanket rolled off him and hit the floor in a lump. He stood, and although he was a young man his body ached. He'd have to rename the chair as he no longer regarded it as a comfy chair.

He shook out the aches and then his eyes fell upon Katie. He whispered her name, although she was snoring away. As if she knew he was thinking of her, she raised her hand. He thought she must be dreaming of school. She mumbled something inaudible, lowered her hand and turned to face the window and went back to sleep again.

Benjamin left her to sleep on, leaving the door ajar so he could hear her if she woke up.

As he moved away from her door, he wondered if she was the kind of kid – like he had been – who became afraid when waking up in an unfamiliar place. Since she'd mentioned her mother left her with others often – but always returned for her – he preferred to err on the side of caution just in case.

In the bathroom he tidied himself up, then set the kettle to boil in his kitchenette. He craved a hot sweet cup of tea, and some buttered toast.

While he waited, he thought about families and how Katie's questions had stirred up some unresolved issues in his mind.

His parents had died, leaving him an orphan. He realized he blamed them for leaving him, even though it was through no fault of their own. As he had no other blood relatives, he went into the foster system. He'd

shut himself off, shielded himself in that system after his first stint had been in abusive home.

After that experience, he'd gone from being a grieving child to a terrified one. Then, instead of moving him to a safe home, they moved him on into an even worse one. And then into another and another. He thought he deserved the bad luck then, but now he knew that he should have been protected there. Instead, he had no one to trust, and he went into fight or flight mode. Being too little to fight for himself against all the adults and other children in the homes, he did the latter. Maybe it was why he felt the need to blame his parents after so many years because he had to blame somebody besides himself.

After he ran, they caught up with him and again, put him in a home where he was abused both physically and mentally. In some cases, he preferred the physical to the psychological. And again, he ran vying never again to trust anyone.

Then, purely by chance he ran into El and Abe. They were out for an evening stroll, holding hands. They were old, perhaps twice the age of his parents. When he opened his heart to them, El hugged him. She fed him. Abe listened. El invited him to come and get a good night's sleep in their spare room. Since then, he never left their home, other than when he moved from the spare room into his own apartment. It was on his thirteenth birthday.

As he stirred his tea and added sugar, he thought of Katie's mother. Had she returned? Would she still be there when Katie woke up? He hoped she would. He hoped she'd be so happy her daughter was safe. So happy and so relieved that she'd never abandon her again. But bad parents were always bad parents. Leopards didn't change their spots.

He imagined Katie's mother finding the doll hidden in the bushes. Would she panic and call the police? His prints would be all over it. Still, he

wouldn't change anything even if he could because all he wanted to do was help her.

Holding his mug, he paced. Maybe he should have taken the child to the police station. Now, he might find himself in bother. Even when teenagers told the truth, came clean – adults didn't believe them. Not if there was another adult involved.

He took another sip, as someone knocked on the door to his apartment. It was Mr. Julius, Abe, his guardian, landlord and boss. "Come with me, shhh," he said as Abe followed him up the stairs to his apartment. Benjamin showed Abe a glimpse of the sleeping Katie. Since she'd kicked the covers off, he tip-toed inside and put them back over her again. Silently they returned to the kitchen.

"Who is she?" Abe asked.

Benjamin hesitated, wondering where to begin. "Her name is Katie, and her mom did not collect her

from the waterfront yesterday. I didn't know what else to do, so I brought her here."

Abe told Benjamin he should have taken her straight to the police station.

Benjamin shook his head. "She was too tired and frightened." He stood up, unplugged his recharging phone, "I can call them now."

"Wait," Abe said. "Let's think on it now she's here." They sipped more tea in silence. "You did the right thing. I'm proud of you."

"Katie and I talked about taking her down to the precinct last night. We decided to wait, give her mother another chance this morning. Also, we left her doll there. It's life-size, one of the Christmas imports you sell."

Abe smiled. "Oh really? I don't remember her, but perhaps El will. Although, I'm sure we're not the only business selling the dolls."

"True," Benjamin said. "More tea?"

Abe nodded then after a moment of silence. "I guess every parent deserves a second chance, but if she doesn't show up this morning, then I'm calling the police."

Benjamin added more tea to Abe's cup. He hesitated, then whispered. "If Katie's mother reported her missing after I brought her here, they'd be looking for me. They might even arrest me if I went back to collect the doll."

"Wait a minute," Abe said. "Did anyone see you?"

"A woman, tried to get Katie to go with her."

"And no one else?"

"An officer chatted with her briefly earlier in the day, but he didn't come back. He didn't see me with her."

"No sense worrying about the coulds and the mights," Abe said. "You couldn't leave her there all night. It's downright neglect, not to mention a crime on the part of her mother. If you ignored the child, then you'd be an accessory." He sipped. "Although you did the right thing, the abduction of said child is also a crime."

Benjamin gulped, "I, I, brought her here, to safety."

Abe patted the back of the teenager's hand. "I know, and you know that, but will the police believe your story?"

Benjamin pulled his hand away by standing. He began to pace. "When she wakes up, I'll take her straight to where her mother left her. I'll explain to her mother. She will understand. I'll make her understand."

Abe also stood. He took his cup and rinsed it out. "That would be brave. But what if the negligent mother accuses you of taking her daughter to get herself

out of trouble? I mean if she did report her missing. Have you considered what would happen, in that event?"

Benjamin sat down, put his hands on either side of his head. "Then what should I do?"

"Go to the waterfront and collect the doll. If the mother is there, then that's excellent bring her back here with you. If not, come back and let me handle it with Sgt. Miller down at the precinct. You remember Alex Miller?"

"Yes. Thank you, Abe."

"You, who," El called from downstairs.

"Come and see," Benjamin said, "come on upstairs." When she was at the top, he put his finger to his lips, "Shhh." She nodded and they tiptoed into the guest room where Katie was still sleeping soundly.

"A child. What on earth?"

"Don't worry, I'll fill her in on the details. In the meantime," Abe said, "you go to the waterfront while the child is sleeping. If her mother isn't there come straight back."

Benjamin nodded. "Thank you, Abe and El. I'll run."

Abe explained everything to his wife. "I'm curious to know if the mother has done this kind of thing in the past."

"That's what I was wondering, too," El said.

Meanwhile, Benjamin ran to the waterfront where he picked up the doll. His phone vibrated.

"Any sign of the mother?" Abe texted.

"No, but I have the doll. I'm coming back now."

Abe sent him a thumb's up emoji. He said to El, "No sign of the child's mother and I need to get ready for the store to open."

"I'll remain here with her," El said. She sat down in the chair while Katie slept on. Sometime later, El went to tidy herself up in preparation of her shift.

CHAPTER TWELVE

KATIE AND BENJAMIN

Katie and her doll were side by side on a huge Ferris wheel, going around and round. When it got to the top, it stopped, while their legs dangled over the edge. She fastened her grip around the bar. For a second, she felt safe and secure. Until the bar dissolved between her fingertips and the car began rocking. Backwards and forwards, then side to side. In the distance, the wind howled, then a dog howled. The doll began to slip. She reached over to grab it, and the cart toppled over, and they fell.

She screamed!

By then Benjamin had returned. He ran into the room. "Wake up Katie," he said. "You're having a bad dream."

Once she realized she was safe, Katie threw her arms around him and held on for dear life. When her breathing slowed, she yawned and said, "I'm starving!"

"Good thing as you're invited for breakfast with Abe and El, come on."

They left Benjamin's apartment and entered the house. In the kitchen Benjamin plopped eight eggs into a pot of boiling water. He asked Katie to man the toaster, as they'd need eight slices.

"I love toast soldiers!" Katie exclaimed. When the bread was toasted Benjamin buttered it. He cut it into strips: the perfect size for dipping into the runny egg yolks.

"What were you dreaming about?" Benjamin asked. "Sometimes it's better to share a bad dream. If you want to."

"I, I don't want to think about it," Katie said settling into a seat at the kitchen table.

Mrs. Julius, El, popped her head into the kitchen. "Hello," she said beaming a smile in her direction.

Katie, pushed back her chair, ran to El and threw her arms around the stranger's waist. Hugging tightly, like they'd met before.

El patted her on the head for a long time, fighting back the tears, then shooed her to the table.

Benjamin looked on, understanding how Katie felt. El, had that kind of face, those eyes, from which kindness, gentleness flowed. He'd taken an instant liking to her himself and now Katie was doing the same.

"Well, I'd better take this to the shop so Abe can have a snack," El said. "You know how much he hates working alone in the shop. Saturday is our busiest day. This treat will be a welcome surprise."

Benjamin brought the eggs in egg cups to the table.

El closed the door behind her on the way out.

"She's a nice lady, isn't she?"

Katie beamed both with her eyes and her smile. "Yes, she's my first instant friend."

Benjamin shook his head. "Instant friend - that's a new one for me." He touched the top of one of the eggs, they were still too hot to crack open.

Katie took in a deep breath, then closed her eyes. She opened them again. "Have I hurt your feelings? Because you and I weren't instant friends?"

Benjamin smiled. "Not at all." He cracked open the first egg. "I just wondered." He put a little butter and salt onto the egg, then cracked open another and did the same.

"I never met my Grandma. El, looked like the Grandma in my head – that's why she's an instant friend."

"Makes sense."

El returned and the three of them dipped their bread soldiers into the runny eggs.

"You're a really excellent cook," Katie said.

He smiled as they cleaned up and put the dirty dishes into the dishwasher. "Let's get moving. Remember, we have things to do."

"And places to see," she giggled.

"I'm glad you're here," El said.

***

Benjamin combed Katie's hair which he noticed smelled like honey and cinnamon.

"I bet my mommy is looking for me. Can we go and look for her now at the waterfront?"

With a smile, Benjamin went out of the room asking, "Haven't you forgotten someone?" He returned a few seconds later hiding something behind his back. "Voila!" he exclaimed as he revealed the doll to Katie.

She threw her arms around its neck, cooing and whispering how she'd missed her twin so much. Benjamin had been right, her doll did smell like Christmas morning, and that was a good thing. What wasn't so good, was she felt a bit soggy in places. She pulled a face.

"Ah, you noticed she's a bit damp," Benjamin said. "Bring her here near the vent and she'll be right as rain in no time at all."

Together they placed the doll near the heater, then Benjamin, suggested. "How would you like to learn to brush your teeth with your finger? That's until we get you a toothbrush?"

Katie squealed and had fun learning. Afterwards Benjamin laced up her sandals.

"Your mommy wasn't there, at the waterfront, when I collected the doll this morning."

Her bottom lip went out. It trembled.

He looked at his feet. "Don't worry. Mr. Julius, I mean Abe, has a friend who works at the police station."

"Oh, no," Katie said.

"What's the matter?"

"They'll find out."

"Find out what?"

"I can't tell you, but I don't want my mommy to get into trouble."

"Don't worry, Abe's friend is a nice man. He'll know how to help. Meanwhile, you and I can hang out with El today."

The child nodded.

"She might even let you help in the store, like a big girl."

Katie smiled. For the moment, she was distracted from her troubles.

CHAPTER THIRTEEN

ABE AND SGT. MILLER

Abe asked his wife to mind the shop and was already on his way on foot to see his friend at the station Sgt. Alex Miller. He'd reconsidered the plan to call him. A visit in person would be better since they were longtime friends.

When they first met years ago, Alex was a young officer and a newbie. Abe had been working in his shop, when two armed men stormed in and stole the cash in the register. Abe got away with a slight knock in the head. He was so grateful his wife had gone to the wholesalers on that day.

After contacting the police, they sent Alex along with a more senior officer. The older officer suggested Abe should hire someone to watch the door. He said it

was either that or pay for an expensive security system. Abe couldn't afford either option. They filled out a report and left, but Alex came back. He offered to moonlight - for a fee. As a young officer, they weren't sending many hours his way.

Abe agreed to pay Alex two hours a day, and they became friends. A few months into the working relationship, another shop on the same strip as Abe's was burgled. Alex apprehended both the criminals single-handedly. Later Abe identified them in a lineup, and the thugs were sent to prison.

After that Alex started moving up the ranks. He and Abe kept in touch though, and when Alex married, he and El attended. When they had their first, child, he and El were invited to the Christening. A little girl followed by two boys–twins. Abe and El, over the years attended Christmas and Thanksgiving in the Miller home.

Then, when Benjamin came into their lives and Alex was promoted to Sargent, they lost touch in regard

to family matters but still managed to get together every now and again for a cup of coffee.

Arriving at the police station, he asked at the front desk to meet with Sgt. Miller who he was told wasn't available. Abe sat in the waiting room for a short while, until he spotted a billboard across the room with photos of children on it. Missing Children.

Abe moved in for a closer look after cleaning his glasses. None of the children had long blond hair. Satisfied the child named Katie wasn't among those on the poster he sat back down again.

Sgt. Miller arrived, and the two friends shook hands. Miller suggested they get away from the station at a coffee shop within walking distance. "We won't be disturbed there, and I could use the break."

They sat in a café booth, Abe asked how everyone was at home.

"It's been a while, old friend, hasn't it? They are well, thank you," Miller said. He opened his phone and showed Abe a short video of his twins' high school graduation ceremony. "Henry wants to be a Doctor," Alex said with pride. "Jimmy wants to be a Lawyer." He flipped through more photos then stopped. "And Jenny, why she and Will just gave us our first grandbaby. She's quite a beauty." He left the photo open for Abe to look at and went back to the preparation of his coffee by adding two creams and a sweetener.

"Ah, she is quite a cutie. Congratulations to you and your wife on being a first-time grandparents." He sipped his coffee. "Oh, and a Doctor is a well-respected profession and going into law is too. Both are safer career choices than your line of work." He laughed then he stirred his cup of coffee.

"That's for sure," Alex agreed as he took a sip. The strong coffee burned his lip, still he took another sip.

"The world is getting more and more dangerous" he continued, "and I hope to retire sometime in the not-too-distant future. Besides, I don't want to be worrying about my sons putting their lives on the line when I can finally put my feet up and relax."

The two friends sipped and dipped their donuts into their coffees.

"So, what brings you down to see me today?" Alex asked glancing at his watch. "I hope that wife of yours isn't causing you any trouble."

Abe smiled. "No." He hesitated. "I have a friend."

"Oh, no, not the I have a friend gag."

Abe continued, "I have a friend," he smiled, "who's in a bit of bother."

"Tell me more."

"He found a child, at the waterfront last night sitting alone. Abandoned by her mother. He took her to safety."

"Your friend is a good citizen," Alex said. "So, in this scenario, how can I help?"

"My friend is wondering, if he could be in a bit of hot water for getting involved in the situation. He's underage and the child was too traumatized to bring her to the precinct. If, my friend came forward now, would he get into trouble for delaying the report?"

Alex considered the matter. "How well do you know this lad?"

Abe sat upright, "You remember Benjamin?"

Alex finished drinking his coffee. The waitress returned, asked if they wanted anything else. When they declined all but the bill, she cleared the mugs away.

"Oh, yes, I remember him. A nice well-mannered lad who appreciates how fortunate he is to be a member of your family."

"He's always been like a son to us," Abe said. "And speaking of family and children, I wondered something."

"I'm listening."

"I saw a program the other night, Matlock, remember it?"

"Yes, it's a bit out of date though – especially his white suits." Miller laughed.

"Yes, I remember when they were popular though – white suits and spats. Yes, I'm that old."

He laughed, then continued. "In the program it said that a person can't report their child missing for twenty-four hours. It's an American show, as you know, but I wondered if it's the same here."

"In Canada, a child can be reported missing any time. There's no waiting period."

"Oh, I didn't know that" Abe said. "Interesting."

"Most people think it's twenty-four hours," Alex said. "This misinformation can be credited to reruns and fake news."

Abe laughed. "Has anyone reported a child missing then, I mean here in town since yesterday?"

"Not to my knowledge," Alex said. "Could be that I don't know about it yet. Sometimes things trickle through at the station." He leaned nearer. "I need to know - where is the child now?"

"Benjamin introduced us to her this morning. El is making a fuss, as you can imagine."

Sgt. Miller nodded as his phone rang. He was needed back at the station.

He asked if a child, a little girl had been reported missing in the past twenty-four hours, none had. He disconnected. "No new reports of missing children."

"Uh, I see," Abe said. "What should we do now?"

Miller said, "If you bring her to the station, we'll take care of her until Child Welfare gets involved."

"She's settled in so nicely with us."

"Yes, leaving her with you right now might be the best option. While we investigate. Would hate to see her shipped into the foster system prematurely. Especially if it's a first offence."

"We'd keep her safe."

"I know you would, but I'll need to check with my boss. From where I'm sitting it's probably best to leave her where she is." He stood. "Anything else you want to tell me, before I make inquiries?"

"Benjamin returned to the waterfront today in hope the child's mother would be there – she wasn't."

"It's a good thing she didn't return," Miller said. "This needs investigating. To see if she's a repeat offender." He checked the time again. "How old is the child?"

"I don't know for certain, but I expect seven or eight."

Miller left the café talking on his phone and returned a few minutes later. "She can remain with you for now. In the meantime, I'll ask my Officers to keep an eye out for a woman wandering about at the waterfront. Any idea what she looks like?"

"No, you'd have to speak to Benjamin. Or I can ask him for you, and let you know?"

"Sure. Find out and text me." He extended his hand, and it was warmly received.

"Thank you," Abe said.

Miller added, "No matter what happens, don't hand the child over. If the woman shows up, stall her, and call me. Anytime twenty-four-seven. I want to speak with her – give her the what for. Also, to make sure she's legit and understands the mistakes she's made. If necessary, I'll get Social Services involved."

Abe said he'd text over the woman's description ASAP.

"Good man," Sgt. Miller said, as they parted outside the café.

Abe, instead of going straight home went to the Waterfront. He sat down on a bench and listened to the seagulls and the waves. After thirty minutes of seeing no one, he returned to the shop where his wife came out to greet him.

"As good as gold," El said as she kissed her husband first on the left cheek and then the right.

He noticed his wife had a spring in her step and her cheeks were flushed. It reminded him of the days when they first courted.

***

After catching up with El about his meeting with Sgt. Miller, Abe asked the children what they were watching on television.

"It's SpongeBob SquarePants," Katie said. "He's funny."

"Uh, you can fill Benjamin in on what happened later, if that's okay? As I'd like to talk to him outside for a moment or two."

She nodded.

"Did you find out anything, down at the station?" Benjamin inquired after closing the door behind him.

"I'll fill you in, in a moment, but right now Sgt. Miller wants me to relay a description of Katie's mother to him via text." He handed Benjamin his phone. "You go ahead and type in the information. You're a faster typist."

Benjamin clicked in: Hi Sgt. Miller. This is Benjamin. Katie's mother wore a dark sleeveless dress, a red scarf, and high heeled shoes. Her hair was dark, almost black and she was wearing dark sunglasses yesterday when the sun was out."

"Height?" Miller replied.

"Approximately 5 ft. 7. – without the heels."

"Thanx. S.A.M."

Benjamin returned a thumb's up emoji. "So, tell me what you found out about Katie."

"At first I brought it up as hypothetical. We talked, then I filled him in on the specifics."

"Okay, fair enough."

"I can confirm," Abe said, "she hasn't been reported missing yet."

"Something must have happened to her mom. I hope she's okay."

"Sgt. Miller, Alex, said you did the right thing by bringing her here. His officers will keep an eye out for the mother. If she shows up, they'll bring her in for questioning. If there is any news about Katie, they'll let us know."

"Thank you again, Abe."

"Since it's Saturday, and Katie doesn't have to go to school, that's a good thing. Hopefully, it will be sorted before Monday and she'll be back in class like nothing happened."

"Yes," Benjamin said, already thinking about how much he'd miss her when she was gone.

El came into the hallway and the trio whispered together.

"We, Abe and I think she'd be more comfortable in the guest room."

Benjamin looked disappointed and his gaze went to the floor.

El touched him on the arm. "I can keep a watch on her when you two are minding the store. We can do girlie things."

Abe interjected, "You need your sleep too, Benjamin, and that old chair isn't suitable for sleeping in."

"We've been meaning to have that old thing replaced for years."

"It's on my to-do list," Abe said. "I'll get around to reupholstering it one of these days."

"Better toss it into the bin or use it for firewood. I've been meaning to fix up the room a bit. Those bookshelves also need refinishing."

"I'll add it to the list."

El kissed him on the forehead. "It would be nice to make the room more girlie."

"She's only here for a short while."

"I know, I know. But it makes me think of my younger sister Sammy. Samantha. The mischief we used to get up to together." She glanced at her husband. "I've always wanted a little girl of my own – this is the next best thing. Even if it's only for a little while."

Abe put his arm around her. "I get it, you two want to play together."

El kissed him on the cheek and the three of them went into a group hug.

When they came apart Abe asked, "Does Katie know her address?"

"She knows it, and we checked it out last night. No one was home and she doesn't have a key. It's on Ontario St., Number 74."

Abe called up Google maps on his phone and put the address in with the plan of going to the house. After he had a look himself, he'd let his friend, Sgt. Miller know the address. "The child will need things," Abe said, giving his credit card to Benjamin. "Buy casual clothes, pajamas, decent shoes, socks and under things. And a toothbrush."

Benjamin tidied up the kitchen while Abe chatted on about his visit to the police station. "Oh, and one more thing, if Katie sees her mother, or visa-versa, she is not to be returned to her. They want a word with the woman first down at the station."

Katie came into the kitchen, "Is my mommy in trouble?"

"No, no darling," Benjamin said. "The police want to make sure she's okay that's all." He ruffled her hair. "Now wash your face and brush your hair." She went into the bathroom and closed the door.

"What if her mother causes a scene? I mean, if she sees me, a stranger with her daughter?"

Abe whispered, "She abandoned her own daughter. Anyone could have taken her, so I doubt she'll cause a scene." He checked to make sure Katie hadn't come out. "Besides, the poor woman may not be right in the head. If she sees the child, ring the police, and stay put. Ask for Sgt. Miller. He remembers you and he'll see to it."

Benjamin sat down and remained quiet.

"I see we've worried you," Abe said. "The child will know what she likes and what she needs, and the staff will assist you."

Benjamin looked at his feet, he knew nothing about buying clothes for a little girl.

El said, "Would you like me to come with you?" She looked at her husband. "If that's okay with you? It's after 3, so, it won't get terribly busy again."

Benjamin nodded. "Please, Abe."

Katie mimicked Benjamin's words. "Pleeeasssse, Abe."

Unable to resist, Abe nodded.

"We're going shopping, for you," Benjamin said. "You, and El and I."

Katie squealed with delight.

CHAPTER FOURTEEN

A DAY OUT SHOPPING

Before long Katie had everything on the list.

"Now let's get something to eat," El suggested.

They went into a café on the main street. Katie ordered a strawberry milkshake, El asked for a strong tea and Benjamin a coke with ice.

She sipped her milkshake. "You want to ask me something, right El?"

El nodded. "How did you know that child?"

"It's okay if you ask me. I don't mind."

El hesitated then asked, "What's your favourite colour?"

Katie laughed, clearly not the question she expected. "I don't have one favourite colour. Why choose one, when there are so many?"

El smiled. Not the answer she expected.

"I have a question," Benjamin asked. He hesitated while both El and Katie waited. "Who bought the doll for you? Was it your mom?"

Katie sipped more milkshake through her straw. "He did," she said.

El leaned in closer, "Your father?"

"No, my mommy's friend Mark. It was a present. He always brings me presents."

"For Christmas? Or your Birthday?" Benjamin asked.

"No, for nothing presents. He just shows up and brings something for me."

"Oh," Benjamin said, glancing at El. "So, how is your milkshake?"

"It tastes like heaven," Katie said, then put her finger over her lips.

"What's wrong?" El asked.

"I'm just thinking..."

"About what?" Benjamin inquired. "You don't have to tell us if you don't want to."

Katie thought about it, then said, "If my mommy was here, she'd be having a caramel milkshake. We'd sip slowly. We always sip slowly. I forgot and sipped quickly, and now it's all gone." She pouted.

"Would you like another one?" Benjamin asked.

"May I?"

"You may." He called the waiter over.

When he arrived Katie said, "Wait, I don't need another one."

"Why not?" El inquired.

"It's simple. Now that I can have another one, this one is enough."

Benjamin and El looked at each other, then back at Katie.

"You're one of a kind, child," El said.

"That's what Mommy always says."

She paid the bill, and they went into the street.

"Can I wear my new shoes, please?"

"Of course, you can," El said, as she removed Katie's sandals.

She wriggled her toes inside the runners then bounced along the sidewalk. El and Benjamin tried to keep up with her.

CHAPTER FIFTEEN

BACK HOME AGAIN

They returned home where they found Abe sitting in a rocking chair. His shoulders were slumped, and his hands were crossed on his lap.

El went to him and kissed him on the forehead. "I'm off to run a bath for Katie. It'll help her to sleep after all the excitement."

"Good idea, love," Abe said. Then to Benjamin, "How was shopping?"

"It was fun – Katie is full of energy. Even I had trouble keeping up with her."

Abe smiled. "Sorry I missed it." He lowered his voice. "I have more information. I'd prefer to share

with you and El at the same time. When the little one is asleep."

Benjamin yawned.

Abe said, "Why don't you go on up, catch a few zzzs. We'll talk in an hour, okay?"

"Sounds like a plan. Thanks." He went up the stairs.

When Katie was asleep, they gathered in the living room. El prepared a few sandwiches. Abe was especially hungry. He hadn't eaten since breakfast.

"She went to sleep straightaway," El mentioned. "And she looked pretty in her new Princess nightie."

"We had a wonderful day today, thank you so much for helping El."

"My pleasure."

Abe finished chewing his sandwich, wiped his mouth and took a sip of water. "I have news. It's not an easy tale to tell. Please don't interrupt or ask questions until I'm finished."

Both El and Benjamin moved in closer and agreed.

"After I closed the shop at 5, I went to Katie's house. I hadn't planned to go until tomorrow, but something made me want to go today and so I went." He paused.

Get on with it, Benjamin was thinking but he knew that saying it would have been rude.

"I knocked on the front door, no one answered but the curtains were open. I stopped and listened for sounds from within, nothing. I went around the side of the house and to the back. There was no sign that a child lived there, no toys, bikes, swings, or balls. No laundry hanging on the line.

"I ordered a taxi, and the driver was waiting for me at the curb. I went next door and knocked. A man answered, told me that someone lived next door, a little girl, and a woman, that's all he knew. Then he slammed the door in my face.

"In my peripheral vision, I saw a curtain move on the other side of the street. I crossed over there and knocked. A woman answered, invited me in for a drink.

She saw the taxi waiting and told him to clear off. Said she'd contact another when I was ready to go. I agreed, feeling she might have information to impart about the child's mother. She was a busy body, of that fact there was no doubt. Normally, I'd avoid her, but in this case information for the child's well-being was key so I remained.

"Her house was clean and tidy. I was not at any risk, and the only sound in her house was the incessant ticking of a grandfather clock. We sat down, shared a pot of tea.

"When I asked about the child, she told me there were always goings on in the house across the street. Shouting. A revolving door of men and cars parked in the driveway and sometimes there was spillover into the street. She figured those were married men. Oh, and she also said the latest fancy man had a big car and a driver. Katie's mother was the talk of the street."

El put her hand to her mouth, "Poor little mite."

Benjamin changed the subject. "Did you find out anything about Katie?"

Abe sighed. "Quiet and well behaved," Judy Smith the neighbour explained. "She said she noticed both mother and daughter yesterday morning. It stood out, because it was a school day and the child toted along a life-size doll with her. She didn't see them return home though.

"When she became bored with talking to me, she went to the front door of her house and whistled down the street. Her son, a taxi driver pulled up in front She shoved me out the front door, into the vehicle and I gave the man a false address. I didn't want them to know my address. They seemed eccentric."

"You mean loony?"

Abe nodded, then poured himself a cup of tea and offered a cup to El and Benjamin.

"You may ask questions now," he said.

***

Minutes passed, perhaps fifteen minutes or more, before El broke the silence. "That poor little mite. What her life must've been like with men coming and going all hours of the day and night." She fought back a sob, deep from within her maternal core. "No life for any child – and here's us. You and I, who could never have a baby of our own."

"There, there," Abe said, patting his wife's arm. "My sentiments exactly. There's no justice in this world. No rhyme or reason. And yet, who are we to judge?"

"All I know," Benjamin interjected, "is that Katie loves her mother."

"Even an abused child loves her mother," El said.

"The proof is in the abandonment," Abe said.

"Maybe it couldn't have been helped. We don't know what happened," Benjamin said.

"That's true. I'm sorry for being so quick to judge. So, what happens now?" El asked.

"We wait," Abe said. "And we ask questions, without upsetting little Katie. Find out what we can. Meanwhile Sgt. Miller will get things moving on his end. I passed on Katie's address; Benjamin gave a description of her mother to him. They'll check the hospitals, the morgue, and the waterfront."

"The morgue," El said. "I don't want to think about that little one being all alone in the world."

"I know, I know," Abe said. He changed the subject. "Oh, and before I forget." He reached into his pocket and pulled out an envelope which he put on the table. "This was in the mailbox at Katie's house."

"Abe, it's a federal offense to steal another person's mail!" El exclaimed. This outburst wasn't enough to stop her from turning the envelope around so that both she and Benjamin could read it.

"I'm fully aware of that fact," Abe confirmed. "But now we know her mother's name is Jennifer Walker."

Benjamin yawned and stood, then kissed El on the cheek. "Katie is not alone now. She's here with us." He said good night. "Thanks for all your help." Abe slapped him on the back like a father would a son.

Upstairs he changed into his pajamas and dropped into his bed. He was too tired to pull down the covers and instead snuggled into the duvet.

***

Benjamin was standing on the edge of the roof of a tall building unable to look down, with his toes already over the line. It was nighttime, and the stars were slits, like eyes in the sky, watching him, willing him forward. Jump, they seemed to say. Just jump.

He teetered and tottered. It was as easy to go forwards as it was to go back, and he was all alone. All alone in the world, with no one to look after him. No one to care for him. No one to care if he lived or died.

He'd read many books, about heroes. Young boys who, like him had lost their parents and done amazing things with their lives. Of course, those kinds of characters were fictional.

Wait a minute! I'm a good person. I help people. I think of others before myself. I don't lie or steal, or hurt others and I always, almost always, keep my promises.

Why almost always? a voice high above him asked.

He didn't answer – instead, he toppled over the edge – and woke up on the floor beside his bed. His clothes were damp with perspiration – but he was safe. Safe and well. Although it was 4 a.m., he wasn't going back to sleep again. He settled in to playing games on his phone. Below his room, he could hear someone pacing back and forth. Probably Abe. He put on his headphones. After a few friends joined in he became totally immersed in a multiplayer online game. He played on until the sun rose on the horizon, then went back to bed.

CHAPTER SIXTEEN

ABE AND EL

Abe couldn't sleep. "Are you awake?"

"I am now."

"I'm a bit hungry, how about you?"

"Now that I'm awake, so am I. Come on I'll fix something. What are you craving?"

As they meandered along the hallway, they looked in on Katie.

"She's such a little angel."

"That she is." Now in the kitchen Abe said, "Toasted cheese sandwich would suit me fine."

"Okay, you put the kettle on, and I'll fire up the grill."

When the food was ready and the tea steeping in the pot, they sat down and ate their sandwiches.

"That really hit the spot, thanks."

"Comfort food always does." She pushed her chair back.

"No, sit for a minute. I want to talk with you."

"Cup of tea?" Abe nodded and she filled their cups. "What's troubling you? I know something is."

"Remember, we talked about adopting Benjamin?"

"Yes, but as he was already fifteen, we decided not to go ahead."

"And yet, I keep thinking if we did adopt him, then if something happened to me – he'd be family and able to help you with the shop. To take over if necessary. Same if something happened to you – he'd be a significant help to me."

El stirred her tea. "Does he want to be adopted? He doesn't need us like he used to when he first came here to live with us. He's an independent young man. I'd hate to chain him to us."

Abe raised his voice. "Chain him to us? Is that what you think? I, I."

"Calm down love. In a couple of years, he'll be old enough to fly away on his own – and he's got every right to go. What was that saying, if you love someone set them free and if they come back, they're yours,"

"And if they don't, they never were. I don't recall who said it."

"Maybe Kipling, or a wise person like him. I'm not saying he'd never come back; I think he would. He loves working in the shop."

"Yes, and one day, he could own the shop – run the shop. Carry on our legacy."

"If he wants to."

"Of course."

"What would you like to do? What will ease your mind?"

"I'd like to talk to Travis our Lawyer, to ask for his advice."

"Shouldn't we broach the subject with Benjamin first?"

"If we did and changed our minds after legal advice – it might have repercussions. I'd rather check first, then we can decide. If we decide to go ahead this time, we can talk with him and see what he thinks."

El yawned. "Oh, excuse me." She took her husband's hand into hers. "Sounds like we have a plan. Now let's go back to bed, that little one will be up soon wanting her breakfast."

CHAPTER SEVENTEEN

I MISS...

Abe and El finally fell asleep when Katie let out a shriek down the hall.

El was by her side in seconds, almost like she'd anticipated it. The minute Katie saw her, she threw her arms around her neck.

Abe arrived shortly thereafter. "Now what's the matter little one?"

"I miss..." is all she said before pressing her face into El's chest.

Benjamin stumbled into the room. "Whatsamatter?"

Katie remained still, while they exchanged soft whispers.

"She misses her mother," El said. Katie snuggled in closer. "You two go back to your beds, and I'll remain here with the little one." Then to Katie, "You'd like that now, wouldn't you? If I stayed here?" She whispered something to El. "Oh, I see," she said. "Are you sure?" Katie nodded. "She'd like you to stay, too, Benjamin. Grab a blanket from outside and you can throw it over yourself on the chair over there." Benjamin followed her instruction.

"Well, good night then," Abe said, as he closed the door, happy to return to the comfort of his own bed.

CHAPTER EIGHTEEN

SUNDAY, SUNDAY

Sunday mornings were special in the Julius' household. Since the store didn't open until noon, the family always prepared and shared a big breakfast.

"It's waffles today," El announced, pulling the waffle iron out and plugging it into the socket. She went ahead and prepared the batter until the grill was ready.

Meanwhile, the others set the table. Condiments such as: syrups, fruits, butter, and whipped cream in a can were all placed upon the table.

"Waffles smell so good," Katie said, as El placed the finished waffles in the centre of the table.

"Thanks love," El said. "Anything we forgot, before I sit down?" No one could think of anything, so she took her seat at the one end of the table while her husband was at the other.

"Thank you for the gourmet food," Abe said, which was his version of a mealtime prayer. "Now, dig in!" And they did.

Katie sat and observed the others since she'd never had a waffle.

"What are you waiting for, love?"

"I'm watching since the only waffle I've ever had was an ice cream cone."

"That's a clever idea," Benjamin said. He went to the freezer and pulled out a container of Neapolitan ice cream.

Then he grabbed the ice cream spoon from the drawer and brought them to the table.

El helped Katie to put fruit onto her waffle including blueberries and strawberries. She added a few apple slices. "It looks pretty," the child said.

"Now you give it a try," Benjamin said.

Katie added a scoop of ice cream, and chocolate sauce.

"Oh, I just thought of something else," El said, pushing her chair back. She turned to Katie, "You're not allergic to nuts, are you?"

"No. A couple of kids at my school are, so we have to be careful but I'm not allergic to anything."

"Me either," Benjamin said, as he scooped crushed walnuts onto the top of his waffle. Then he added whipped cream – although he, like Katie already had ice cream on his waffle.

"Can I have whipped cream too?"

Benjamin sprayed the cream onto Katie's waffle. "It looks too good to eat now," she said, and everyone laughed. Her face lit up, "MMMMM," she said. "MMMMM."

After each ate their fill, El prepared coffee.

"I'm too full to move," Benjamin said.

"Me too," Katie said, patting her stomach.

Abe looked at his watch, there was still time until the store opened. "Oh, I meant to ask you Katie, what's the name of your school?"

"I go to St. Mary's Elementary," Katie said.

Abe typed the address into Google.

"Do you like school?" Benjamin asked.

"It's okay.

"We'll give your school a call tomorrow," El said, "and let them know you'll be absent for a few days."

"You mean I don't have to go?""No. We want to keep you here for the moment."

"Until my mommy comes back?"

"Yes, until then," Abe said.

"Do you miss school often?" El inquired.

"Only if I'm sick or if Mommy is unwell, because she doesn't let me walk on my own."

"Is your mommy ill often?" Abe asked, thinking about the allegations of alcohol and drugs.

Katie began to cry.

"Enough questions for now," El said. She took Katie's hand into hers. "Let's get the whipped cream and chocolate sauce washed off your face, and get you dressed in your new outfit. Come along now."

Katie followed and when behind closed doors said, "Mommy doesn't want to be sick."

"Of course not, child," El said as she ran a warm damp washcloth across Katie's face. "Now lift your arms and let's get you dressed."

"I'm a big girl."

"Even big girls need a little help sometimes," El said as she winked.

"Thank you."

"Thank you, for bringing a little sunshine into my home."

Katie thought for a moment and then said, "But you already had sunshine, because you had Benjamin."

El laughed. "You're right, we see his golden rays every day. Now come along with you, we can't let the boys be ready before the girls, can we?"

"No way!" Katie giggled.

CHAPTER NINETEEN

SGT. MILLER

When Sgt. Miller arrived at the station there was an urgent message waiting for him from the Coroner:

"A woman's body washed up on the shores of Lake Ontario early this morning, near the Viaduct. Usual suicide haunt. She's down here at the morgue now. She has no identification, but she fits the description of the woman you asked me to keep a look out for. Should have the cause of death verified soon. Come on over when you get in, I'll update you then."

Miller immediately went to the morgue. The body was on the slab and the coroner and his assistant took down information.

"You might want to have a look at this," he said, pointing to the cut across the woman's throat.

"Suicide is out then," Miller suggested, "based on the angle of the blade she couldn't have done it to herself."

"Exactly," the Coroner confirmed. "And we also found traces of skin and hair under her fingernails."

Miller looked at the woman's nails, painted in cardinal red. Looking at her face he saw a smudge of the matching lipstick remained on the corner of her upper lip.

"We already sent samples along to the lab. Should be able to I.D. her and possibly her assailant if we find a match for either on the database."

"Mind if I take a sample of her fingerprints, so I can run it through our database when I get back to the office? Might be a quicker path to an I.D. if she's been booked on any criminal offense."

The Coroner nodded.

"What else do we know about her?"

"Age is estimated between 34-37 oh, and she was multiparous."

"Two births," Miller said. "Can you tell when she had the kids?"

"C-section. Seven maybe eight years ago. Vaginal birth recent."

"Anything else?"

"We estimate the time of death on Saturday night, between 7 and 9 p.m. No alcohol or drugs were found in the body." He hesitated, "One more thing, she had bites on the back of her legs." He turned the body. "See here and there, bites. Snapping turtles could be the cause, but the bites are large."

"I see," Miller said. "Thanks." He paused. "What's that, near the spine?"

"A birthmark."

It was about the size of a loony.

Miller left the building and the sunlight hit him with full force. He put his dark glasses on and kept walking to his vehicle thinking about the child staying with Abe. Hoping the dead woman and the missing mother weren't the same person, but his gut told him otherwise.

CHAPTER TWENTY

LEGAL EAGLE

Abe was up and out of the house before the others woke. After his conversation with El, he set up an appointment with his old friend, also their lawyer Travis Anders.

"I'd like you to go ahead and draw up the papers. When Benjamin turns twenty-one, he'll inherit the house and the shop."

"Whoa, slow down there. What about El?" Travis said.

"We can help him in the shop as required. But he'll have an incentive to step up, get more involved since it'll be his one day."

"El needs to be here too. The house and shop are in both of your names."

"If you put together the forms for us, I'll bring her in to sign them. We've already discussed it."

"What's the hurry?"

"No hurry as such. Just want to get the ball rolling. How long will it take for you to have everything drawn up?"

"Give me a week," Anders said. "Then you must come back with El. Have you discussed it with Benjamin already?"

"Not yet. I want to see how it looks on paper. How it all fits together before we get him involved."

"I'm happy to take your money, Abe, but if I draw up the papers and he refuses, you'll still have to pay my fee."

"I understand. Wouldn't want it any other way."

"Okay, Abe. Leave it with me. I'll get in touch when it's ready and you can bring El." He hesitated.

"I'd discuss it with Benjamin in the meantime, even if it's a hypothetical situation."

"Once signed, it will be official?" Abe asked. "What if we change our minds?"

"I'll include a Codicil. In case you decide to rescind the offer in the future."

"Thank you, Travis."

"Oh, and you aren't legally bound to reveal the Codicil to the boy, unless you choose to. Also, when we bring the papers to him for signing, he should have his own lawyer present. If he can't afford it, suggest he contact Legal Aid for help. We can talk about that when we meet, I can fill him in or recommend another lawyer. We'll need to give him a little time before he signs."

"Benjamin is like a son to us," Abe stood, "and I want to make this easy for him."

"Hold on now Abe, please sit down," Travis said. "I'm your lawyer, but I can't represent both of you. It's for his own protection that he gets counsel other than me."

"We've known each other for twenty-five years," Abe said. "I trust you. The boy can't afford another lawyer. It seems ridiculous for me to pay someone else when I trust you."

"I will explain all to him one-on-one so he understands and can ask questions without you or your wife present. The Codicil is for your and El's piece of mind. It's not a reflection on the boy, it's a matter of law. Putting everything in writing, is for the protection of everyone involved."

"I value your advice," Abe said. He paused.

"Which reminds me, I was watching reruns of Matlock the other night."

"Used to love that show," Travis said. "Please continue."

"Well, in the episode, they tried to force a spouse to testify against her husband. Chaos ensued, but Matlock had it thrown out of court."

"Ah, that Matlock. Rules have changed since then. In Canada today, a wife can be subpoenaed to testify, but she doesn't have to disclose anything. Not if it occurred during the time they were married. It's known as marital privilege, Section 4, Canada Evidence Act."

"Interesting indeed," Abe said. "How does it work with children? Can a parent be forced to testify against a child or vice versa?"

"There's been plenty of discussion over this through the years."

"And what does the law say?"

Travis went to his bookshelf and flipped through until he found what he was looking for. "It is the basic right of a child to be heard in any preceding. That's Article 12, from The United Nations Convention of Rights of the Child. Ratified in 1991." He closed the book and put it away. "Any other questions?"

"No, thank you for your time." Abe stood and extended his hand.

"I'll be in touch," Travis said.

Abe made his way home. Having someone there to look after his wife after he'd gone was his number one priority. Nearly home now he wondered if Sgt. Miller had any news to share. With this situation, no news was good news. Finally arriving home, he went inside.

CHAPTER TWENTY-ONE

SGT. MILLER AT THE PRECINCT

Sgt. Miller watched as men and women in handcuffs paraded into the station. He felt like he was in the middle of a bad reality program.

"Was it a party?" he asked the arresting officer.

"Yes, a street party on the east side. Drugs and alcohol everywhere."

A woman caught his eye, as he signed a form. She was blond, with a noticeably too short skirt and too much makeup. She blew him a kiss. He turned his back on her. Better the cadaver than that for a mother.

He wondered was any mother better than no mother at all. It was like the question if a tree falls in a forest does anybody hear? There were no correct answers in theory, but in reality – no mother had to be better than a few he'd encountered.

He went back to his office just in time for the results of the print scan for the woman on the slab. Sure enough, she was on the database, but she hadn't always been a local. She was from Quebec. He wondered what she was doing in town. He continued searching for information and found a Missing Person Report. Yes, it was the woman on the slab. He flipped through the file, checking into her background. Then called one of his friends over in Montreal. One of the guys who didn't mind conversing in English – and filled him in on the details.

"A woman's body was just found, based upon a Missing Person Report filed through your office it's Marie Levesque," Miller said.

There was silence on the other end, before Office LaPlante asked, "Cause of death?"

"Her throat was cut, but it's as yet to be determined if that was cause of death."

"I'll let him know. He's working with the Ontario Provincial Police."

"He's a local officer? I can get in touch if you'd prefer. Tell him anything he wants to know and where to come to identify the body. I can be there with him if he wants me to be. If he doesn't have family here."

"She was all he had," LaPlante's voice wavered. "He was working under cover."

Miller hesitated. "Could this murder have anything to do with his investigations? Has his cover been blown?"

"Uh, I don't know. I'll run it up the flagpole here. I'll find out what I can, and you do the same on your end. You have connections in the OPP?"

"Sure do, I'll be discreet."

"Thanks, Alex."

"Sure thing."

Miller hung up, but kept the phone pressed against his ear. He rubbed his chin in the place where his beard used to be. He missed that beard, but his wife sure didn't.

At least it wasn't little Katie's mother, but it was still a murder. With the OPP involved things in the city might get a little more complicated. He dialed Abe's number and waited while it rang several times.

***

"Hi Abe, it's Sgt. Miller, Alex here."

"Hello."

"Just calling to see how Katie is doing?"

"Yes, Katie is settling in fine," Abe confirmed. "Any news on her mother?"

"We have a few leads, nothing certain though."

"Can I help?"

"We'd like more information on her, like her last name."

"It's Walker, I found that out from talking to one of her neighbours."

He sat down. "When?"

"On Saturday. While El took her shopping for necessaries and I went along to have a look."

"I'm guessing Mrs. Walker wasn't home?"

"No sign of her or anyone else. I had a chat with the neighbours."

"Did you pretend to be one of us, I mean, a Cop?"

"Me? Don't think I could pull that off, I'm way too short," Abe said. Both laughed. "Don't worry, I was discreet."

"Anything pertinent you want to share?"

"Uh, well, lots of men. One neighbour said it was like the house had a revolving door. Said the mother was the talk of the street–and not in a positive way."

"Interesting. Did you sense animosity or anything close to a motive?"

"No, not at all. She's nosy and bored – but not likely a murderer. The woman I spent the most time with was fond of Katie. She saw them leave the house. Wondered why she was bringing her doll to school. She never saw them return home. My assessment was, this woman knows everything going on, on the street with everyone."

"Okay, Abe, thanks for letting me know. Stay clear of the area now though, leave the investigating to us."

"Uh, if you and the officers are going out to the house, I'd like to come along with you, if I could."

Miller took in a deep audible breath. "It's not standard procedure, to bring a civilian along and it will take a while to get a warrant. We'll probably have to break down the door."

"I'd still like to be there. I promise not to get in the way – and the neighbours have seen me, know me."

"As it's you, I guess I can make an exception if you promise to remain in the vehicle until I tell you otherwise. I'll give you a buzz once I've applied for the warrant and a team to come along. If you're ready, you can join us. If not, we'll make our way to the Walker residence without you. Clear?"

"One hundred percent," Abe said, smiling down the phone. He hung up, then turned to his wife who was busy brushing Katie's hair, "I might have to go out as soon as the phone rings."

"Has this anything to do with Katie?" Benjamin asked. He had been watching television.

Abe moved closer to him and whispered, "That was Sgt. Miller on the line. They don't have any definite news."

"Can I come along?" Benjamin asked.

"Unnecessary, but thank you," Abe said. He lowered his voice to a whisper, "Sgt. Miller didn't want me to tag along, but I insisted. Between you and me, we're going to investigate her house."

"Okay let me know what you find, In the meantime, I'll manage things here. Maybe take Katie out for fresh air." Benjamin stood up and said, "Anyone up for going for a walk?"

"Me!" Katie squealed.

"Me too!" El said.

They left and Abe sat beside the phone waiting for Sgt. Miller's call.

CHAPTER TWENTY-TWO

CASING THE JOINT

Miller updated the Chief of Police about Katie's situation. While he waited for the search warrant, he organized two officers to accompany him. He called Abe, "We'll be at yours in ten minutes, are you ready to go?"

"Ten-four," Abe replied.

The officers sniggered behind Miller.

"He's a good man," Miller said, as he pushed the gas pedal to the floor.

Abe was extremely excited to be a part of the sting. He smiled as the cruiser pulled up to the house. Miller stepped out and handed him a bullet proof vest which he put on under his shirt.

While he was doing so, Miller introduced him to Officers Belago and Rippon. He shook their hands. He wanted to let them know that Abe Julius wasn't a pussy.

Abe moved to go into the back seat, but the two officers gave way so he could get into the front. "And no, you can't play with the siren," Miller said. The officers chuckled.

Miller had a bit of a lead foot and one officer in the back said so. He laughed. "I'm still your boss, even with a civilian in the front seat. At the house, the three of us will go in. Abe as agreed you will remain in the vehicle."

"Yes, I understand, but let me know if you need my help."

"Uh, yes." Then glancing in the rear-view mirror, "Once we're in boys, we'll have a quick look around. As usual, put your gloves on and remember don't touch or move anything.

"As we discussed, a photograph of the mother and daughter would come in handy. Also look for one with the father in it."

Abe shifted in his seat. He'd love the chance to have another cup of tea, and chat with the nosy neighbour.

"I'll leave the radio on when we go in so you can listen to some tunes."

They stopped at a jammed intersection. A multi vehicle fender bender was blocking traffic. Miller put the red light on with the siren and parted the way, after he asked if everyone was okay.

"Will you let me borrow that sometime?" Abe asked, rolling down the window.

Everyone laughed as Miller said, "No way."

"We're here," Officer Belago said.

Miller turned the volume up on the radio. "All set, Abe. You stay here and sit tight."

"I'll protect the vehicle," Abe said.

Sgt. Miller put on his gloves. "Let's go boys."

Sgt. Miller knocked first, then rang the doorbell, while Officers Rippon and Belago kept an eye out. When no one answered, Rippon went around the right side of the house, while Belago covered the other side. They returned in a few moments.

"All clear," Belago said.

"All clear, Boss."

"Okay, let's see if we can get in without breaking down the door," Miller said.

Belago removed tools from the trunk of the car. They jimmied the lock in no time at all.

Miller stuck his head inside and called out, "Hello? Anyone home?"

Hearing nothing, they made their way inside with weapons at the ready. The only sound was the refrigerator buzzing. Miller opened the door to find it stocked with food, condiments, and several bottles of uncorked wine.

"Doesn't look like someone who planned a trip," he surmised.

Belago and Rippon investigated the ground floor.

"All clear and secured," Belago reported.

On the fireplace mantlepiece in the living room family photos were on display. "Take that one," Miller said, pointing to a photo of a little girl and a man. Abe hadn't mentioned a father. In fact, the neighbour had told Abe the house had a revolving door of men. Who was the guy in the photo with Katie then? After looking at all the photos on display he was surprised there were no mother and daughter photos.

The officers followed Miller up the creaky carpeted stairs.

"Hello, Police!" Miller called out, with his weapon aimed ahead and ready for anything. Anything but what assaulted his nose. The unforgettable stench of death.

The officers involuntarily gagged, as they continued making their way to the top of the stairs. Now on the landing the reek was unbearable.

In contrast to the stink, the first room on the right was a child's room, all done up in pink, with ruffles on the bed and flowery wallpaper.

As they continued, the stink grew worse and their eyes filled with water, "This is not looking good, Boss," Belago said, then he held his breath.

"It isn't smelling great either," Miller replied as he moved on toward the room at the end of the corridor.

It turned out to be the master bedroom with the door standing wide open and inside, in the bed there was a dead man.

And it wasn't just any dead man. It was the man they'd just seen downstairs in a photo on the mantlepiece with the little girl.

He was under the covers, but the torso and lower body looked strange, or to be more specific they were aligned strangely. Upright, but not straight. He threw back the covers.

"Jesus," Officer Belago said observing the man was sitting beside himself.

"Now why would anyone sit someone up like that after they cut them in half?" Miller asked.

"There's no blood in here," Rippon observed, "and no bloody trail."

Fleshy tendrils emanated from both halves of the torso.

"Rigor mortis has set in, explains the position – somewhat," Miller said. "I'll call it in, you two check around for the weapon." Then he spoke into the phone again.

"Yes, this is Sgt. Miller. We need a full forensic team down here. And backup to secure the property. Also, the Coroner, an ambulance, one body bag. Oh, and tell them not to use the sirens - we don't want the entire neighbourhood coming out to see the show. Yes, ten four."

"Boss, we found something," Belago called from the down the hall.

The bathroom was a bloody mess. In the bathtub: a chain saw. Bleach had been poured on it, to mask the smell of all the blood.

"He was definitely cut here," Rippon said, covering his nose with the back of his hand.

"Bleach, blood and air freshener, a lethal combination," Miller said, fighting back a heave.

He called in again, "Tell the forensic team to come in full gear." Then to the officers, "Let's see what evidence we can put together before the others arrive."

"What about your friend in the car?"

"He'll stay put, until I tell him otherwise."

"Not the curious type?" Belago asked.

"He's curious alright, but he knows when to draw the line."

CHAPTER TWENTY-THREE

THE BODY

They returned to the room with the body when Miller's phone rang. It was The Chief of Police asking for more details about the murdered man. "He's been dead for a couple of days, mid-thirties, male, caucasian."

"Any idea how he died?"

"Yes. We found a buzz saw in the bathroom. He was dismembered in there, then moved in two parts into the bed. They went to a lot of trouble draining the body first and putting the segments under the covers on the bed. It was like he was sitting beside himself."

"Sounds like someone with a strange sense of humour."

"A mother and child live here. This guy was in a photo on the mantlepiece with little Katie. I don't see how a woman could have done this thing, without help."

"Sounds like a two-person job, at least. Fill me in when you return to the station."

"Will do," Miller said, then disconnected.

"Sarge," Rippon whispered, "this guy looks kind of familiar."

"He was in the photo downstairs."

Miller laughed. "I agree, he does look like someone. Maybe he's from a prominent family?"

"Hello!" a woman's voice called from downstairs.

"Jesus, now who's that?" Miller asked, going out to the top of the stairs.

The woman in the foyer fit the description of the "nosy neighbor" Abe said he spoke to. He leaned over the banister.

"Please leave the premises immediately."

She didn't move like her feet were cemented into place. She started to babble, "so worried about that little girl, poor thing."

He started down the stairs, "You need to go."

She jumped.

"Thank you for your, uh, concern, but we need you to go, now." He led her out of the house and onto the front lawn. He glared at Abe, wondering why he hadn't stopped her from going in, then remembered he'd given his old friend specific instructions to remain with the vehicle no matter what.

Miller returned inside the house and locked the front door behind him. He'd come down when the forensic team and the others arrived and let them in rather than take a chance any of the other neighbours might venture inside.

Judy Smith sniffled into her handkerchief on the front lawn, then spotted Abe in the cruiser. She waved at him and he waved back.

She then moved across the street to the front yard of her own house and stood there gaping.

It wasn't long before several vehicles filled the driveway and lined the streets.

"Nothing to see here," one said to Judy Smith.

Abe watched everything going on around him, dying to know what was happening. What had they found inside? Was Katie's mother dead? They'd taken in a stretcher for someone. Perhaps she was injured? And Judy Smith had walked right into the house, bold as brass. If only he could get out and ask questions.

He continued watching, as they cordoned off the property with that yellow tape he'd only seen on television. And the team of people who went in wearing masks and gloves – they were forensics. He'd seen them on television too.

Feeling like a gooseberry he was glad when Miller got back in the car again.

They drove on – for the entire journey Miller did not utter a single word. Not even a good-bye when Abe got out of the car.

***

On the way back to the Walker house, Miller went over what he knew. He was grateful Abe hadn't pelted him with questions.

As he parked down the street from the house, he got out of the car. He noticed a curtain shift, wondered if that's where the nosy neighbour lived. He knocked on the front door and flashed his badge.

"Sgt. Miller," he said. "Sorry about earlier, but civilians aren't allowed at the uh, scene of the crime."

"I understand," she said. Then leaning in close, "I never miss an episode of CSI and I've read every single Agatha Christie novel."

He smiled. "Mind if I ask you a few questions?"

"No, I'd be happy to help. I'm home all the time with mobility issues. Come on in and take a seat." He followed her into the sitting room. Her chair was half pointed in the direction of the television and half pointed in the direction of the street. The room had a faint smell of cigarettes and VapoRub. The hefty woman dropped rather than sat in her chair.

Miller let her get settled in, then asked, "When was the last time you saw anyone come or go from the house across the street?"

She folded her hands and put them on her lap. "On Friday morning, the little girl and her mother left, later

82

than usual."

"Katie is her name, isn't it? And her mother is Jennifer?"

"Yes, that's correct. And they were dragging along that doll."

"Anything else about Mrs. Walker? We heard she returned to the house, after she went out but without the child."

"Not that I saw." She stopped. "Oh, come to think of it, I had a quick shower." She hesitated, then leaned in closer and whispered, "I'm not one to tell tales, but one thing I noticed about Mrs. Walker was on that morning, she was wearing a wig. I thought where on earth is that woman going with her little girl dressed in those sparkly sandals, carrying a doll on a school day? I thought maybe she was taking it for show and tell, but that's only for younger children." She hesitated.

She glanced out the window, as a car drove by then continued. "And her all dolled up like that and wearing a wig? Why none of it made an ounce of sense. And there was me, thinking about that poor little girl.

"I've lived on this street all of my adult life I've seen lots of strange things. I'd need plenty of time to tell you all of it." She took in a deep breath. "But you're not interested in all of it, you're interested in the Walkers. Let me just say, on that morning, it was the first time and probably the last time that I'll ever see such an unusual trio walking along our street."

"A wig eh?" This was new information. He took out his pen and paper.

""Yes, it was odd. Besides the wig, Katie was wearing sandals, inappropriate for school. Why, when my boys went to school sandals like that wouldn't have been allowed. There were rules to follow. Everything changes, always for the worse." She huffed. "Besides, that child was struggling to keep up and they'd only just left the house and she had that doll in tow."

"What about the day before, did you see or hear anything?" He knew her type. Abe was right. Judy Smith had nothing better to do than to poke her nose into everyone else's business. It wasn't exactly a quality he looked for in a friend, or a neighbour, but in this case, she might end up being his only lead.

She thought about it. "The day before, nothing. No one came or went." She hesitated. "The day prior to that one though, I remember something. Would you like a cup of tea?" She turned her body a little to watch a cat walking by.

"No thank you," he said. "Please continue."

"On Thursday, I was outside getting worms for my son."

He looked up from his notepad.

"My son fishes on his day off. The doctor says it's fine, me collecting worms."

He nodded. "Just the facts, please." He so wished she'd get to the point.

"I heard shouting and raised voices."

He sat up, now interested again. "A woman's? A child's?"

"A woman, yes. And man."

He nodded for her to continue.

"I finished getting the worms and everything went quiet. I returned inside."

"Any idea who the man was or when he arrived?"

She frowned. "Men came and went in that house. I'd need an extensive list to keep track." She picked up a paperback novel and fanned herself. "Oh, I do remember something else. It just came to me. On Friday around midday, when she returned – Ms. Walker, a car was waiting. She let it into the garage."

"Then what happened?"

"I fell asleep. I sometimes sleep here in my chair. But I heard it, distinctly – a droning sound. Like a lawnmower, or."

"A saw?"

"Could have been a saw."

"Oh," he said. "Did you see the vehicle leave?"

"No." The front door screeched open, then slammed shut. "Charlie?" she called out. Charlie was her taxi driver son, and after the introductions she filled him on the conversation.

"I came home for lunch on Friday afternoon," he said. "Mom had nodded off in her chair, but the sound woke her. I heard it when I was walking from my car. Definitely sounded like a power saw to me."

"You're both certain of the time?"

They nodded.

Upstairs, Miller heard a chair scraping against the floor. "Is there someone else in the house?"

For the first time, the woman seemed nervous, and she wrung her hands as she spoke. "Yes, that's my other son. I'll be up in a minute!" she shouted, without attempting to stand.

A sound, like that of a wounded animal rang through the house. After two attempts, she was on her feet. "They say he's not right in the head, but he's still my son."

"It's okay, Mom," Charlie said, patting her on the arm as she walked by.

"I'd like to meet him," Miller said.

"Sure thing - come on up," Judy said, as she mounted the first stair while holding on to the railings on either side. Miller brought up the rear. When she reached the top of the stairs, she knocked gently before entering. "We have a guest here to see you, love, he's a policeman."

Miller nudged his way in and extended his hand to the man – who did not return the favour. Instead, he sat with the fingers of his right hand on the keyboard of a small laptop. The man looked out the window, as a car went by and clicked on the keyboard.

He crossed the room to have a closer look. The man was typing in the license plate number of the cruiser outside. Not just the cruiser, but every vehicle he could see. "Are you interested in vehicles, or license plate numbers?" he asked.

"No, No, Noooo!" he cried, bashing himself on the sides of his head with both fists.

"Gerald, now you stop that!" his mother said, grabbing both of his fists then after he'd settled down kissing him on the forehead as she let them go. "The nice man was only showing an interest in your work."

Gerald tapped away on his keyboard.

"We're going now, don't you be rude and embarrass your mother anymore. You keep up the excellent work." She closed the door behind them. On the stairs she said, "He has issues."

"Don't we all," Miller replied. Now back in the living area, Charlie was no longer there.

He waited for her to sit, before he sat down himself. "You called what he was doing work, what did you mean?"

"Ever hear of the term hexakosioihexekontahexaphobia or triskaidekaphobia?" she asked.

"Afraid not. But phobia stands out. He has phobias, what's it about?"

"He's afraid of numbers like sixty-six and thirteen. There's no rhyme or reason as to why. When he met with a psychiatrist, she suggested he keep a record of letters or numbers. He records license plate numbers, they are easiest for him to see as he's in his room most of the time."

"It might be beneficial to us, to see what he's recorded. How long has he been doing it?"

"Years, and yes, that could be arranged, if it would help."

"Not sure if you know, but Jennifer Walker is missing. Any information on the comings and goings would be helpful."

He handed her his card. "There's my email address. If you can send me the file, it doesn't have to be fixed up or pretty. I will let my people go through it and see if there is anything we can use."

She took him to the door and waved goodbye. As he walked away, Miller saw the curtains upstairs open a little then close again.

That young man upstairs had a treasure trove of information. Possibly a record of every single license plate number for every vehicle that ever arrived on the street.

He wondered if the neighbours knew, they and their guests' vehicles were being tagged. He smiled. If they knew they certainly wouldn't like it – and it was probably against every privacy law in existence. Still, he had a murder to solve and a missing woman to find – and he'd use any means he could get his hands on to find the underlying cause of it.

As he drove back to the station, he thought of how easy it was for Abe to find the nosy neighbour. He had good instincts and picked up on it quickly, and it was his first time visiting the neighbourhood. It was a fair assessment, that all the neighbours knew of Judy Smith's habit of poking her nose into their lives. Was that why whoever cut up the body, had left it there under the covers Instead of disposing of it?

He returned to the station. No matter how hard he tried, he couldn't get the foul stench of death out of his nostrils. He checked his email, nothing from the Smith woman yet.

With no messages or any new information to follow up on, he walked over to the morgue. If nothing else, he could update them on the latest information - Jennifer Walker had been wearing a wig. Now he'd have to widen the scope.

There's not much else he could do until they positively I.D.'d the dead man. He wished he could remember where he'd seen him. The memory was just beyond reach.

One thing he knew for certain the man was up to no good.

CHAPTER TWENTY-FOUR

ABE AND EL

When he returned home, Abe went straight into his office. He needed alone time to process everything he'd seen.

"Knock, knock," El said, as she entered. "You look troubled, love," she gently massaged her husband's shoulder.

"Just thinking," he said, as he straightened up in the chair. El continued massaging his shoulders then her hands moved to his neck.

When her fingers began to hurt, she asked, "Would you like a hot cup of tea?"

Abe stood. "I would, but I'll get it myself." He left the office.

El trailed behind him, "Why don't I make one for you? I could sure use a cup of tea, too."

"No, let me," Abe said as they neared the kitchen. El followed close upon his heels.

"Will you stop fussing!" Abe said, rather more loudly than he expected to.

"Is everything okay?" Benjamin asked.

El said, "Everything is fine. We're deciding who makes a better cup of tea. So far Abe thinks he's winning. Now, go on back to watching your game."

Benjamin and Katie bored with television turned it off and set to playing a game of checkers.

"Don't let me win this time!" Katie said.

"I never!" Benjamin said, over the clanking and clashing of cups and saucers in the kitchen.

A few moments later, El popped her head into the living area. "Who's winning?" she asked.

"Shhh," Katie said. "He's concentrating."

Benjamin smiled.

"It's a lovely sunny day out there and I think you two should go out and get some fresh air. Or maybe, kick around a ball!"

"That's a clever idea. Come on!" Benjamin said.

"He's only saying that because I'm winning!" Katie cooed, as she followed him out the door and into the back garden.

From the liquor cabinet in the corner of the same room, El poured a shot of Abe's favourite fifty-year-old Scotch into a glass. She added a spritz of soda. She carried it to him.

"I thought maybe something stronger might settle your nerves."

He smiled and thanked her, touching her hand. "I'm sorry, El."

She kissed him on the forehead, then went to the kitchen window which looked out on the garden. El laughed and soon Abe joined her. Together they watched the two children running and playing in the garden.

Abe took a few sips and relaxed, hoping the body bag he'd seen at the house hadn't contained the dead body of Katie's mother Jennifer Walker.

CHAPTER TWENTY-FIVE

SGT. MILLER

Miller arrived at the morgue and had a brief chat with Head of Forensic Pathology J. T. Patterson, who then had to leave him to attend to an identification.

Moments later the autopsy technicians arrived with the body bag from the Walker home. Attached was an Identification Sheet and container marked Personal Effects. A photographer took photos as the seal was removed. Then the body was placed on the examination table. Miller stayed out of their way, while the body was unwrapped by the dieners.

Patterson reentered the room and pulled him aside. "An OPP Officer is upstairs in the viewing room. He's just identified the body of his wife."

"Levesque?" Miller asked.

"Yes, do you know him?"

"No, but I'm the one who reported the body and based on information I saw on the database I thought it was her."

"Would you mind having a chat with him? From up there you will be able to see everything going on down here. It'll be a while before we start the autopsy."

"Sure thing."

"Once we start, feel free to ask questions. We will be able to hear and answer you, albeit our answers might not be immediate. Our priority is the person's body."

"And rightly so," Miller said. Then he left the room, stopping briefly on the way to get a cup of hot tea from the vending machine. He handed it to Levesque, introduced himself then said, "I'm sorry about your wife."

"Merci. She was everything to me, mon monde entier. Our children didn't make it either. It broke her heart. That's why we moved here, for a change of scenery and to begin again." He fought back a sob, then took a sip of the hot tea. "Good," he said.

"I'm very sorry."

"Thank you."

Miller and Levesque sat side by side as the staff below prepared to begin the autopsy.

"We can go somewhere else?" Miller said.

"No, that's not my wife. I'm okay."

Patterson returned to the autopsy room below, dressed in a scrub suit, surgical mark, gloves, and high black boots. Miller and Levesque watched as they took samples and put them into containers which were, then placed into biosafety cabinets.

When it appeared, they were finishing up, Miller asked, "Uh, what do you know so far?"

"Thanks for waiting," Patterson said. "Based upon the bruising around the nose and mouth, and the bloodshot state of his eyes, death by suffocation is highly likely. We need to wait for the blood samples to come back from the lab to confirm it though."

"So, he was dead, before he was cut in two?"

"I'd say so," Patterson confirmed.

"I know this man," Levesque said, nearly spilling his cup of tea which he now placed on the ledge.

Miller moved closer. "Who is he? I recognize him, too as did my officers but none of us could recall where we'd seen him."

"His name is Mark Wheeler. We've been investigating him and his associates in the drug selling trade. He's the son of F. D. Wheeler, the billionaire and media magnate."

Miller remembered now; he'd met both father and son at fundraising events. "Does the name Jennifer Walker mean anything to you?"

"Yes, she was his latest conquest – his bit on the side. What happened to her?"

"We found him like that in her house and she's missing."

"Is she a suspect?"

"Definitely. And get this, his body was cut in half with a saw. Positioned in the bed, like he was sitting beside himself."

"Sounds like a statement."

"A statement made by whom? And for whom?"

"That I do not know," Levesque said.

Miller added. "Jennifer Walker had a little girl; did you know that?"

"No, I did not. Is she missing too?"

"No, she's safe, but no sign of her mother. And that house was a mess. She can't go back there."

Levesque stood. "I'm sorry to hear this, but they are waiting for me at the funeral home. If I think of anything that will help, I'll let you know. Thank you for your kind words, and for the cup of tea." He tossed the empty cup into the bin and left the room.

Patterson seeing Levesque leave said, "I'll call you when we know anything for definite. No point in sticking around. It'll be days before the lab gets the results back on some things, others, maybe hours if we're lucky."

"Thanks."

Miller returned to the station and clicked Mark Wheeler's name into the data base. There was loads of information about him, both good and bad. Mostly bad though, as he was well into the drug game. He spent the afternoon filling in reports and sent a couple of officers out to let the next of kin know.

Miller busied himself around the station, checking to see where he was needed, when several hours later Patterson called. "Results just came in: cause of death was suffocation. I was right – he was dead when they cut him in half."

CHAPTER TWENTY-SIX

HOME SWEET HOME

It was close to midnight. The house was quiet except for one sound, the sound of Abe's bare feet slapping on the hardwood floors as he paced back and forth. He was mostly dressed, bar his socks and shoes. He sighed, put his hands behind his back and walked. Then turned and paced in the opposite direction.

El, was in her nightgown, patting cold cream onto her cheeks and forehead. She propped her pillow up and grabbed a book of Mary Oliver's poetry from the night table and began to read. Even though Mary was her favourite poet, El simply could not focus on the words or rhythm of the lines.

She closed the book, pulled up the covers and watched her husband walk up and down. Finally, she asked, "What's the matter my love?"

Abe stopped for a second, then went right back to ambulating.

"Tell me. You know what they say about a problem shared."

"I can't."

El turned the bed down and stepped into her slippers. She led Abe by the hand and set him down on the end of his side of the bed. She kneeled, cradling his head between her hands, then went on to massage his temples. Abe resisted at first, mostly because he was over tired, but soon his breathing calmed. She undid his buttons and took off his shirt, then replaced it with his nightshirt. She attempted to undo his trousers.

"I can do the rest myself," Abe said, as he undid his pants, pulled down his underwear.

El picked up the dirty clothes and put them into the laundry basket. When she returned, Abe was standing like a little boy waiting for his mother to tuck him into bed.

"As you wish," she said, leading him by the hand, fluffing his pillow, settling him in under the covers.

"Thank you, love," he said, yawning.

El returned to her side of the bed and removed her slippers. She slid in under the covers, or tried to, but as always, her husband was hoarding most of the warmth.

She quietly shifted her pillow, tried to resettle, but couldn't. Instead, she listened to his breathing change, and then she knew he was sound asleep.

The moonlight was coming in through the curtains, casting a magical shadow on her side of the bed. She dozed off, remembering the day when she first met her husband.

She and her father were working in the family business. They sold fabrics from around the world and every accessory they could get their hands on related to sewing. Her father prided himself in selling the latest and most up to date sewing machines. Her mother, who she had no memories of had been the inspiration for the store. Her mother had died giving birth to her sister.

When they first started the business, she and her father did most of the work. Her sister helped when she could. Their best sellers and most sought-after fabrics were the ones imported from Asia and Europe.

Then one day, a fabric salesman came in: Abe. Her father had met him at a buying conference in New York. He spoke highly of the young man, saying he was born to be a "fabric toucher."

"The lad has a knack," her father said. "A god given gift, to feel quality and to recognize trends before they become trends in the fabric industry."

"Why don't we hire him, father?" El asked.

"I don't think we can afford him. But I've invited him along for dinner. You can cook your special fried chicken, biscuits, and mashed potatoes. We can find out if the way to a man's heart is really by feeding him."

She laughed, but she was excited to meet this new man. This Abe, with the gift.

That afternoon, he arrived in the shop. She suspected it was him, almost immediately. He was a little over 6 ft tall, dressed in a grey suit which moved on him like a second layer of skin. His blond hair was slicked back, tidy, with not too much oil. She was drawn to him, like a bee to basil, as she watched him run his fingers through their most expensive selection of imported fabrics.

Her father strode across the store to meet him. "Welcome, Abraham" he said as they shook hands. "This is my daughter, El."

"I prefer to be called Abe," the young man said.

El blushed, she'd never heard anyone disagree with her father before. Even today when she thought about that moment, her cheeks grew warm.

Then there were other moments. More powerful moment when she got goosebumps on her arms. It was a magic connection. They were made for each other. As a wedding present her father gave them the shop.

Two years later her father died, and her sister moved away to start a family with her husband. Meanwhile, she and Abe kept the business going, through very tough times.

El, who'd always wanted children was unable to fall pregnant. After tests were completed it was confirmed she was unable to conceive. She worried about disappointing Abe, but he didn't mind – or if he did, he didn't let it be known to her. The business became their baby.

Then, after they'd been married for nineteen years, a young lad walked into the shop. Abe watched the ragged looking youngster, expecting him to steal something, ready to call the police.

El observed, "Look, he's a fabric toucher too."

They approached the boy, who immediately burst into tears.

"Would you like a cup of cocoa?" El asked.

He nodded and followed her into the kitchen, with Abe trailing behind. She made him a cup of hot cocoa with two slices of buttered toast and they sat together at the table.

The boy reached out for a slice of bread, then looked at and hid his filthy hands.

"The bathroom is just down the hall," El said. "You can freshen up in there."

While he was gone, Abe said, "I hope you haven't bitten more than you can chew, love. It's obvious he's on the run. He smells and – shouldn't we call the police and let them find out who he is?"

"He's little and harmless. See if he wants to tell us about his plight first. We might be able to help."

"As you will," Abe said as the boy returned with clean hands and a sparkling clean face.

He ate the toast first, then blew on the hot chocolate and downed it. "Thank you."

"Oh, you're welcome," El said. "Is there anyone you'd like us to call, to come and collect you? Your mother or father?"

He burst into tears. "They're dead."

El went to him, and she threw her arms around him, as he explained about the car accident, about foster care, about everything bad that had happened to him. Most of all, how he couldn't go back.

"I have a friend, down at the precinct," Abe said. "He might be able to help."

El held the boy in her arms, while they waited for Abe's friend. "He's a kind man," she said. "He'll know what to do." The boy nuzzled into her.

Sgt. Miller arrived sometime later, by then El had already offered up the spare room to the lad, until something more permanent could be sorted out. That's how they became a family.

Now they all relied upon each other and the store didn't sell fabrics anymore. Still, she had two fabric touchers in her life, and who knows when their talents might be needed again. She knew everything was cyclical.

El looked down at her sleeping husband. She kissed her finger and pressed it to his forehead, careful not to awaken him. He smiled, just as Katie let out a scream down the hall.

CHAPTER TWENTY-SEVEN

KATIE

"Katie," a voice whispered. "Katie."

"Mommy, where are you?"

The little girl rubbed her eyes, at first unable to remember where she was. She threw back the covers and stepped onto the cold floor. Then scooted across to the other side of the room and turned on the light. Now she made her way toward the window where the curtains were swishing about.

"Mommy, is that you?"

The vent in the floor under the window, the warmth emanating from it, drew her to it like a magnet. When she stepped upon the vent, her nightgown ballooned around her, filling up with warmth from the heat.

"Katie," the voice whispered again. "Where are you, Katie?"

"I'm coming, Mommy," she said, trying to look out the window, but it was too high for her to reach.

"I'm waiting for you," her mother said. "I'm waiting, here."

Frantic to see her, the child searched for something to stand upon. She removed a vase with sunflowers in it from a table, dragged it under the window. Pushed the bed next to it. Stood first on the bed, then the stool. Parted the curtains. It was pitch black in the street below other than the glow of streetlights.

"Mommy!" she called, trying to open the window. When she couldn't reach the top lock, she balled up her fists and pounded on the glass.

"Katie," her mother whispered. "Katie."

"Wait, Mommy, please wait for me."

She stepped off the table, onto the bed, onto the floor, and went to the bookshelf. She lifted a bookend in the shape of the letter A with two hands. She placed it on the bed, while she climbed onto it. Then placed it onto the table, while she climbed up on it. She lifted the A and hurled it at the glass.

The glass shattered both in and out, catching her and the area surrounding her with shards.

"Mommy!" she cried.

She was still sound asleep, shaking, looking out of the shattered window.

CHAPTER TWENTY-EIGHT

EL AND KATIE

El and soon Benjamin made their way along the hallway into the little Katie's room. When they found her, lit up by the moon, in a ball on the floor near a toppled table. Her blond hair and nightgown moved together like the breeze from the window was one with the little girl's breath. They noticed blood pooling around her. Like a ghost rising in the night, she stood up and called out, "Mommy!"

"Careful, don't wake her," El whispered.

They watched as the tendrils from the curtains floated toward her. The look on her face, the blank stare into nothingness frightened Benjamin. For a few seconds he forgot to breathe.

The moon shadow drifted over her. It accentuated her injuries. It was like she was on an island, surrounded by glass.

Benjamin pushed by, "Stop, don't move," El whispered, but he didn't listen. He swept across the floor and pulled Katie into his arms. Her body went limp. He stood there waiting, unable to move from fear whispering her name.

El returned, carrying the first aid kit.

He placed her on the bed.

"Put warm water in a bowl for me." He didn't move. "Benjamin, warm water. And a facecloth and towels."

He nodded and left the room, while El assessed the situation. She trained as a nurse, a long, long time ago, before she met Abe. She hoped she could remember what to do.

The sound of blood droplets, pitter-pattering onto the clean white sheets pulled her out of her head. She set to working on the wounds using tweezers to remove the small shards. Katie remained asleep.

"She must've been sleepwalking," Benjamin whispered.

"Hold her steady, so I can check for glass pieces and remove them."

"Should we call 911?"

"I don't think so," Fl said, "I think we can manage." She continued, until all the wounds were disinfected and wrapped.

Katie whimpered, but did not wake.

CHAPTER TWENTY-NINE

BROKEN GLASS

"We need to turn her onto her side, now," El said.

Benjamin propped Katie up on her side, while El examined her feet. Only a few glass splinters had broken through the surface of Katie's feet. Most were simply stuck to the skin near the surface and easy to get out.

Her breathing became more rapid on several occasions, but she didn't open her eyes. El put a warm cloth onto Katie's feet and wrapped them now that the bleeding had stopped. She then elevated both feet on a pillow.

"I'll remain here all night," El said. "I don't want to chance leaving her on her own, or of waking her when I get up from the bed."

Benjamin went to have a closer look at the broken window. At first, he thought someone had tried to break in, then he saw the bookend on the floor. He picked it up and put it back on the bookshelf. "I'll be right back," he said.

He went into the basement. He found a sheet of plastic suitable to be masking taped across the window until they were able to fix it. After he taped it up, he swept as much of the glass away as he could.

Exhausted, he found a spot at the end of the bed and fell asleep.

The wind whistled through gaps in the masking tape every now and then, but none of the three sleepers were roused by it.

CHAPTER THIRTY

WAKEY-WAKEY

The sound of a blue jay singing outside the bedroom window caused Abe to open his eyes. He yawned and stretched. Noticing his wife wasn't there he called her name. When she didn't answer, he saw her slippers were missing. "El!" he called as he made his way down the hall.

Arriving at Katie's room he paused and looked inside. El was there, and Benjamin was too.

"El?" he whispered; she didn't wake.

It was then he heard a whistling sound followed by flap-flaps. He tip-toed toward the window to investigate.

The curtains were askew while the glass had been temporarily mended with plastic and masking tape. Unable to make any sense of it, he left the room, closing the door behind him and went to the kitchen.

The sun was rising in the deep blue sky, as he filled the kettle and watched a new day come to be. Now on his to-do list was calling the insurance people to come and assess the damage, but first, he needed to find out what happened.

His stomach rumbled, so he popped two slices of toast in and pressed the lever down. On the way to the fridge, he grabbed a mug and spoon. While the kettle was finishing, he took the milk and butter out of the refrigerator and popped a teabag into his mug. He poured in the steaming hot water, just as the bread finished toasting.

"Morning," Benjamin slurred.

"Morning, son," Abe said.

Something inaudible from Benjamin.

"Sit right now, the kettle's hot and I'll pour you a cup of tea."

Benjamin obeyed without speaking.

"Want a slice of toast?"

The teenager nodded.

Abe removed his toasted slices and popped down one slice, then another. He put a tea bag into a second mug and poured in water, stirring it so that it steeped super-fast.

The older man knew time was of the essence here otherwise Benjamin would fall asleep again – then he'd be useless for the rest of the day. When it was ready, Abe lifted the tea bag out of the mug, added two sugars, followed by a splodge of milk.

Abe took the boy's hands which were resting on the table and put them onto the mug of hot tea one by one. He watched as Benjamin smelled the steaming brew and came alive, before taking a sip.

Seeing the lad was now properly awake, Abe went to finish preparing the toast.

Abe watched, as Benjamin changed, returning to the land of the living a bit more on a minute-by-minute basis. Meanwhile, he drank his tea and ate the rest of his toast.

Moments passed, where the sun came in through the window and danced upon the young man's profile. When he seemed like he could carry on a conversation, or maybe it was hopeful thinking, Abe asked, "Are you going to fill me in on what happened in Katie's room last night!?"

"No."

"Well, I never."

"Not unless you tell me what happened at Katie's house yesterday."

"Oh, I see you are even more awake than I thought you were," Abe said laughing. "But I can't."

"And why not?" Benjamin said as he bit into the toast. The crunchiness and salty butter tasted so good.

"Because my old friend Sgt. Miller swore me to secrecy. If I could tell you, I would. Now, you tell me what happened with that window. I need to call the insurance people and I can't do that until you tell me what happened."

Benjamin continued eating his toast.

"So, you want to play the question game? Question number one, did someone try to break in and take the child?"

Benjamin who had now completed his tea and toast, leaned back in the chair, putting his hands behind his head.

"I think she must have been sleep walking. From what I could see, it was the bookend which was used to smash the window. I can't for the life of me figure out why though. None of it makes any sense."

"The poor child. Why didn't you wake me?"

Benjamin leaned back further, so the front legs of the kitchen chair lifted off the ground. "Sgt. Miller would never know you told me anything."

"Trust is trust. You either do it or swear to it. Or you don't. It depends what kind of person you are. I keep my word and so does my friend. Sgt. Miller and I, trust each other and like you and I, we keep our word." Abe refilled his cup from the teapot. "To be honest, I know very little. He even made me stay in the car, out of harm's way. I can only surmise what I know from the comings and the goings, but I don't want to pass on any misinformation."

"You must have seen or heard something," Benjamin said followed by a slurping sound. He knew Abe had no intentions of breaking his friend's confidence and changed the subject.

"It all happened so fast, with Katie. She screamed and we ran in. She had glass pieces in her feet. El got them out. I didn't know she had training as a nurse and it sure came in handy. We managed the situation and there was no point in waking you."

"Was she badly hurt? I saw blood on the floor."

"El confirmed her injuries were minor. Katie slept through the whole thing, while El pulled out the glass shards with tweezers and even when she put disinfectant on the cuts."

"Have you noticed," Abe said, "the child doesn't laugh much? She giggles occasionally, but she doesn't laugh, as a child should laugh."

"Everyone is different, perhaps she is just shy."

"There is also sadness. I mean behind her eyes. Something familiar and yet, arresting."

"Can't say I've noticed anything like that, are you sure you're not imagining it?"

"I saw that look once, when you first came to us," Abe offered.

"Me?"

"Maybe not fear, maybe sorrow or sadness, but it was constant, pain, remorse, neglect. All rolled into one. It is still there in your eyes, but your soul is also bending out a stream of light which overpowers it, whatever it is. You have found yourself, conquered it, found your own truth. But little Katie needs to be healed, cared for as I cared for you."

Benjamin put another tea bag into his mug, stirred it a few times, then removed it, added sugar and milk, then took a sip. "She and El have a bond."

"You're right about that and I'd best get ready to open the shop. Let me know when breakfast is ready," Abe said placing his dishes into the sink and went to get ready for work.

In the family room Benjamin turned on the television. Immediately he recognized Katie's house. There were cameras, media everywhere. The property was cordoned off by yellow police tape. Something bad had happened there, he already knew that. Now he would find out what. He turned up the volume. Moved closer.

The reporter wearing a navy-blue power suit and dark-rimmed glasses stood near a white van upon which bore the initials for the local television network were displayed.

"This is Carly Wright, reporting from Ontario Street where a body was discovered recently. The man has been identified as Mark David Wheeler. His immediate family have been notified. The police are looking for any witnesses who saw him go into this house behind us whose residents are Jennifer and Katie Walker. (She held up two photos.) Both are missing and were last seen near the waterfront on Friday morning."

Wait a minute, Katie's mother had blond hair in the photo. When he saw her, her hair was black – was she wearing a wig on that day at the waterfront? And if yes, why?

The reporter continued. "Mark Wheeler comes from a well-known family in this region. A family who has helped many charities over the years. Details of funeral and visitation to follow. If anyone with information on Mrs. Walker or her daughter, please contact your local police or give me a call."

He wrapped his arms around himself thinking of a dead body in Katie's house. His entire body started to shake. To get his mind off the news, he went back into the kitchen and plugged in the kettle. While it boiled, he looked out the window.

The sun rays kissed the pavement, as squirrels lifted leaves while birds flew in and out of the feeder. They had no idea a murder had been committed, or a little girl had woken up screaming with glass shards embedded in her skin. Their lives went on, in the same way, no matter what was happening to the humans in houses which fed them.

When the kettle whistled, he turned off the burner but did not make another cup of tea. Instead, he continued to watch the normalcy outside the kitchen window, not thinking about anything else until he no longer felt the urge to shiver or shake.

CHAPTER THIRTY-ONE

KATIE AND EL

"Mommy! Mommy!" Katie screamed with her eyes still closed.

As the morning sun streamed in through the flapping plastic, El held Katie in her arms. "It's going to be okay, little one."

Katie opened her eyes – she wasn't at home and she wasn't in her own bed. "Mommy!" she called. "Where's my Mommy?"

El let her go when she pulled away.

Benjamin who'd heard Katie's screams took over. "Katie, you're fine and everyone is looking for your mommy. Remember El? And, remember me, Benjamin?"

Katie reached out and took Benjamin's hand then El's. She cradled them against her cheeks as the tears flowed down, then she noticed the bandages on her hands. She kicked the covers off and saw the protective wrappings on her feet. "What happened?"

"We were hoping you could tell us," Benjamin replied.

Katie kicked her feet, as she struggled to remove the bandages. When they became loose, she tried to remove the ones on her hands. El grabbed her hands and put the covers back over her feet and hummed to calm her down. Within minutes Katie was slumped against her shoulder and resting quietly.

A few moments later Katie said, "I remember hearing my mommy calling me."

"In a dream?" Benjamin asked.

El tucked Katie's hair behind her ear.

"Did I do that," the little girl asked. "Did I break the window?"

"Hush now child," El said. "Benjamin fixed it up, and it'll be back right as rain soon. It doesn't matter how it was broken. All that matters to us is your safety. Windows can always be repaired."

"But not me?" Katie asked.

El hugged her. "You're perfect just the way you are."

Benjamin asked, "Can you remember anything? Anything at all about the dream?"

"Mommy was calling me, that's all I remember."

The trio sat quietly. El was thinking about what might have happened. Benjamin was thinking about how glad he was she hadn't been taken or hurt badly. Katie was wondering where her mother was, and what they were going to be having for breakfast.

"I'm hungry," she said, patting her growling stomach.

"Benjamin's piggy-backing company at your service," he said.

Katie wrapped her arms around his neck, holding on tightly and off they went to the kitchen.

"Would you like to be my little pancake helper?" El asked. Katie nodded and smiled; Benjamin found a spot for her on the countertop. "It's a secret family recipe," El said as she broke two eggs into the flour and began to stir. When it was ready, she used a ladle to pour batter onto the hot grill. "Okay, time to flip them over. See how they are bubbling?" She helped the little girl to flip the pancakes.

"It's easier than I thought it would be," Katie said. "Especially with these big oven mittens on."

"Did you ever help your mommy cook?"

"Sometimes, but she never let me sit on the countertop or flip pancakes."

"Cooking can be fun."

"Not cutting up the the onions – they make me cry and I don't like how they taste either."

El laughed. "I'll show you a secret sometime, how to cut them under water, so you don't cry." Then to Benjamin, "Nearly ready, can you let Abe know?"

Katie laughed. "Cutting up onions in the bathtub? That's funny El. My feet would get all stinky."

"No, silly. I mean in the sink. You are right though, if you did cut them up in the bathtub, you'd definitely get stinky feet and stinky everything else."

Katie and El giggled, while they set the table together. Soon Benjamin and Abe joined them. Everyone ate their fill then Abe said he had to return to the shop.

"I'll clean up," Benjamin said. "But it would take half the time if you gave me a hand."

"I guess the customers can wait," Abe said.

"Let's get you dressed," El said to Katie and they left the kitchen.

When they were out of earshot Benjamin said, "We need to talk, Abe."

***

"**W**hat's up?" Abe asked.

"A man named Mark Wheeler was found dead at Katie's house. It was on the news."

"Ah…"

"Is that all you have to say?"

"I need to think," Abe said. "Might as well work while we tidy up."

When everything was back in its place, Benjamin went into the living room and clicked on the television.

"Better close the door," Abe said, which Benjamin did.

"I thought you needed to get back to the shop."

"I do, but in passing I saw the news was on. He moved across the room and turned up the volume.

"I could have done that with this," Benjamin said holding up the converter.

"Already done," Abe said, sitting down.

A different reporter who resembled Clark Kent stood on the front lawn of the Walker property.

He said, "Mark Wheeler's family are well known in this community. Over the years, their generosity has touched and improved many lives through donations to charities and foundations. However, allegations of a connection to drugs, are under investigation."

"Oh no," Benjamin said.

"Shhhh."

The reporter continued. "We are looking for the residents of this house behind me. Jennifer Walker and her daughter Katie Walker." He held up a photo. "If anyone has seen or has any information on the whereabouts of Katie and Jennifer, please call us, or get in touch with your local police."

"What if anyone saw us, shopping with Katie?"

"Shhh."

"Anyone with information about Mark Wheeler, can call the confidential hotline. The number is on the bottom of the screen." He held up the photo again of Jennifer and Katie. "It's imperative we find these two, before any harm comes to them. Please, if you're out there and you have seen or know anything about their whereabouts – call the police. Any information at all might be helpful. Even information which seems insignificant to you might give us some clues so that we can help them. Doug Falcon reporting from SJB TV."

Abe and Benjamin were silent for a few minutes. Then Benjamin remembered that Katie's mother had dark hair on the day he saw her, and, in the photograph the reporter held up, she had blond hair. Benjamin filled him in on this recollection.

"Yes, that nosy neighbour I spoke with, Judy Smith mentioned the wig."

"You mean you already told Sgt. Miller about it?"

"I didn't, but I probably should have."

"You definitely should fill Sgt. Miller in about the wig. But what if anyone knows Katie is here with us? What if, that's why the window was broken last night? Katie said she heard her mother calling. Was she out on the street, below Katie's room calling for her?"

Benjamin jumped up.

"Stop," Abe said. "First of all, you said the bookend was used to smash the window from the inside. Katie was probably having a nightmare. Besides, Sgt. Miller knows we have Katie here with us and he wouldn't let that information get out to anyone."

"Still, we've been taking her all over the place. To the store, to a café. Someone is bound to have noticed. She is a distinctive looking child."

"You sit down here and don't you worry. I'll give Sgt. Miller a call, better yet, I'll pop down there and have a word with him."

He headed toward the door. "In the meantime, remain indoors and tell El to keep the store closed today."

"What reason should I give her? Should I explain everything we've learned about Wheeler?"

"Absolutely not. Make sure if the television is on when Katie is present, it is never tuned into the news."

"Will do."

CHAPTER THIRTY-TWO

DOWN AT THE STATION

Abe walked to the police station where a Press Conference was in progress. Sgt. Miller was at the helm. Miller stood behind a lectern while the microphone was raised to his height. A gaggle of reporters pushed in wielding cameras. A reporter shouted out a question. Abe elbowed his way through the media circus to get up the stairs and into the building. He hated crowds, and being in the centre of this utter chaos was not a place he wanted to be. Miller acknowledged Abe's presence with a nod as he swept by and into the building.

A reporter shouted, "What about the missing child? Any leads on her?"

A second reporter called out, "What do you know about the little girl and her mother? How were they involved with Wheeler?"

Miller held up his hand to quieten the unruly crown. When they'd settled down, he replied, "One question at a time please. First, the child has been reported missing – she's not missing. In fact, we know where she, where Katie Walker is – she is in the safe custody of foster care."

An audible gasp from a woman in the crowd. For a few seconds, a blond woman stood out from the others. He looked away for a second, and she was gone.

"Has Katie Walker been examined by a doctor?" another reporter asked.

"All in appropriate time," Miller replied. "We need your help to find the child's mother. We have zero leads."

Remembering Katie's mother was blond not dark haired as was originally reported – he scanned the crowd for the woman he'd caught a glimpse of before. No such luck. He couldn't see her anywhere.

"I'll take one last question and don't waste it asking me where the child is, all I can tell you is she is safe and well." He chose the next reporter to ask a question, "Go ahead, Maggie." He'd known Maggie from the local paper for years. She wasn't like the others. She was a real journalist.

"Good morning, Sgt. Miller," Maggie said.

Miller nodded.

Maggie asked, "As the child, Katie is in care, why did you take so long to go to her home and investigate?" Although Maggie didn't move, the surrounding journalists did. They jostled and pushed, clamoring to get closer.

"Well Maggie," Miller said. "The child, I mean Katie Walker was abandoned at the Waterfront on Friday. Her home address was only brought to our attention yesterday."

"Untrue," another reporter cried out.

"That's enough," Miller said slamming his fist down on the podium and backing away from the microphone.

The same reporter shouted, "We spoke with the neighbour, a Ms. Judy Smith. She confirmed an elderly man had been to the house the day prior. The same man who she saw yesterday sitting in your police car."

Miller continued walking, ignoring the hubbub, happy the reporters weren't smart enough to put two and two together since the man they were talking about had just slipped by them and into the building.

Before he entered the station, he turned to the reporters. "You had your questions. Now, let us complete our jobs and you do yours. Help us find the child's mother. Thank you for your time." He pushed through the revolving doors and went to his office.

Abe who'd made himself at home by sitting, stood now to shake hands with Miller. Abe said, "We saw Katie's photograph on television and heard about the dead man's body. What a gruesome find. No wonder you were so quiet when you drove me home."

"All in the line of duty," Miller said. "Coffee?" Abe declined with a wave of his hand. Miller continued, "The reporters are hungry for a story, any story. You didn't hear the last question. That woman – your nosy neighbour - mentioned you visited the house and were in my cruiser. When you leave, we must make sure you get home with no one following you."

"Oh no," Abe said. He looked across the desk at his friend. He looked like he'd aged in the last few days. "Have you slept at all? You look like hell."

"Sleep? What's that? I've been trying to put the pieces together here, it's a difficult case. We thought we had a lead on the mother, but it didn't pan out. It's like she vanished without a trace." His phone rang. "Okay, thanks for letting me know."

"No new leads?"

Miller leaned in closer. "That was the coroner. A new body. No I.D., yet."

"What's your gut feeling? Is she Katie's mom?"

"I can't say because I don't know."

"And the dead man, who was he? I mean, I know the name. He's affiliated with drugs. I can't believe any mother would put their child in jeopardy like that."

"Allegedly. Who knows why people do what they do? When we were at the house there was a photo on the mantlepiece of Katie and Mark. Seems odd a mother would allow it, if she was intending to kill her boyfriend." He paused, afraid he was saying too much, then changed the subject, "But, yes, his prints lit up the system. It's the motive we're stretching to find."

"A motive, like a mob hit?"

"Uh, don't let your imagination run away," Miller said. "As for a motive, that I don't know." Sgt. Miller lifted the phone receiver. When the receptionist answered he said, "Yes, I need to have a civilian escorted from the building."

He listened, then replied, "Yes, the back door. Ensure he isn't followed."

Abe stood, "My dear friend, you are coming with me. I bet your wife and kids are missing you and you need to sleep."

Sgt. Miller agreed with Abe in principle, but he had too much to do. Still, he took time to ensure his friend was safely out of the building and on his way home.

"The coast is clear," the driver said. Miller closed Abe's car door, watched until the car was out of sight, then returned to his office.

CHAPTER THIRTY-THREE

BLOND FLASHBACK

It was a fine Sunday afternoon and families were strolling about. Many were picnicking, others were exercising or lounging near the waterfront. The air smelled sweet, as it does when spring is turning to summer. The birds chirping and flitting about were visible on nearly every tree.

In the backseat of a taxicab, a woman observed the city activities. She wished she had enough money to live here too. Now stopped at a red light, she observed a family tossing a frisbee back and forth. When the light changed and the car rolled on, she continued to watch, until she could see them no more.

In her mind, she was going over what she would say to her sister. She'd asked for money before, and her sister had given it – but reluctantly. Mostly because she knew where the money would go which was to pay off her drug related debts. Her older sister would give in, eventually. Still, she hated to be in the position of having to ask. Especially in person. She hoped to get a glimpse of little Katie when she was there, maybe even an introduction. Now that she was seven, maybe she'd even remember her.

Once or twice the driver glanced back at her in the rearview mirror. She adjusted her mirrored sunglasses and wiped away a tear discreetly.

"What are you looking at?" she asked.

"Nothing," he replied, turning onto Ontario St. "What number were you looking for again?"

It was the house surrounded by police tape, with cruisers all over the place.

"Drive on!" she ordered. "Drive on!"

"Ok, but where to now, lady?" he said making a U-turn.

"Just drive, let me think!" the woman exclaimed. She pulled her phone out of her brown bag and hit the speed dial. It rang and rang and rang. She disconnected, digging her fingernails into the armrest. She took a deep breath and hit another number on speed dial. Like the first it went unanswered.

"Lady, I need to know where I'm heading."

She shrieked, "Just drive, until I tell you to stop."

"Okay lady, you're the boss." He drove on aimlessly, stopping and starting when the lights changed from green to red. "We'll take the scenic route."

Back along the shores of Lake Ontario they went. Seeing the money meter and the cost that was going up, she checked in her purse for cash. Her credit cards were already maxed out. "Where's the police station?" she asked.

"A few blocks away."

"Take me there," she said. On the way she'd think of what to say, what to tell them about herself. She spotted a crowd blocking the front of the precinct all the while wondering if this had anything to do with her sister's house.

"Just let me out, over there," she demanded handing the driver a fistful of coins and a few scrunched up bills.

She flattened down the front of her dress now clinging to her with static. Behind her, she heard her sister's name, and Katie's. She pushed forward, waiting to see what the man at the podium would say.

When he revealed that her daughter was fine and with a foster family, she nearly fainted. She took a few deep breaths and left the area, happy in her own mind that her daughter was well. On the question of her sister being missing, well, that would all be sorted out in time.

She kept on walking in the opposite direction to which she'd come. Wearing five-inch heels, she was ill-equipped for a lengthy jaunt anywhere. The breeze caressed her bare arms and she was glad at least there wasn't any chance of rain tonight.

The smell of steaming hot beef burgers, sweet onions and greasy fries nearby made her stomach growl. The perfect hangover food. Virtually penniless now the inhalation of calories would have to suffice. To distract herself she tried recalling the numbers of those who she thought might help her, but the result was the same.

Two doors down, she found a secondhand thrift shop. In the window, there was a blond girl, dressed it seemed for a party. She looked at the face of the mannequin, imagining what her little girl would look like now. It had been years since she'd seen a picture of her.

She'd been blocking it out – as she always did when things became too much for her. "Compartmentalize." That's what her shrink always told her to do. But the house...she'd seen it, cordoned off with yellow tape – police tape – like on CSI or Murder She Wrote. It was her sister's house. Her sister who was the mother to her child. A child no one knew about.

A few doors down a crowd gathered. She joined them, seeing a news program with subtitles. A photo of her sister and daughter under the heading, "Missing Persons." Then a photo of Mark Wheeler under the heading, "Murdered, Drug Connection."

The two incidents were connected. Now her knees really gave out and she slipped down onto the pavement.

"I'm okay," she said, as strangers helped her up onto her feet again. She thanked them and with shaky ankles wobbled away.

She'd heard of this Mark Wheeler through the drug world. Now he was dead. How was her sister linked up with him? Was she, herself the connection? She owed them money. She said she'd repay it. It wasn't even that much. Her sister had repaid her drug debt once, twice – she'd lost count of how many times. Surely, they wouldn't have gone for her sister. Thank goodness they didn't know Katie was hers. If they hadn't known, then how had Wheeler ended up dead? Did that connection bring thugs to her sister's home?

She tried not to think about it, stumbling along to god knows where. Strung out, partly delirious, she remembered the day Katelyn was born. She was young, seventeen, too young to be a mother, and yet when she saw her daughter for the first time, she felt all the maternal feelings which a mother should feel.

Being seventeen was old enough to birth the baby and to raise the maternal instincts, but not enough to convince her to keep the newborn. To raise her. But, oh, that little face. The smell of her. The smell of pink. She cradled her phone in her arms as she trod along.

With tear-filled eyes, she told herself to snap out of it. She'd done the best thing for Katelyn at the time, by giving her to her older sister to raise.

Lost, nowhere to go, no one to talk to, she recriminated herself for coming to town. For being a drug addict. For going to her sister's house. For everything – the whole damned ball of wax.

A man who smelled as bad as he looked bumped into her.

"Watch it!" she exclaimed causing the poor man to burst into tears. She reached into the bottom of her handbag, finding a few stray coins and a throat lozenge, and put them into his hand.

"I thank you," the man swaying to and fro. He blew on the lozenge and popped it into his mouth then asked, "Are you lost?"

"I'm new to town," she said. "Are there any sights to see around here?"

He put his hand to his chin, as he looked her over. "There's a famous Viaduct up there, keep on going and you can't miss it. It's an amazing view."

"Thank you," she said, as she walked away.

Looking forward to seeing the landmark, she opened her purse. She pulled a cigarette out of the packet and lit it. Taking a long drag helped to ease her mind. She thought about what she ought to do, but no answers came.

***

Katie's biological mother had stopped to rest her feet. The park itself was fully active, with children and dogs running willy-nilly. She fancied another cigarette but did not light one. Instead, she listened to the laughter. For in truth, she had nowhere to go.

Her phone vibrated; it was Anson. "Where are you?" he asked.

"I'm near my sister's place but she's not home."

"Well, I have your order ready. First you must pay what's owed. When will you be back to pick it up? I can't keep it here for too long. If you can't pay, then I need to sell it on to someone else. I've a waiting list you know."

"I can't get back straightaway, but I need it. Uh, any chance you could come and get me? I'd pay you back. I'd do anything."

Splat! A child, a little boy's ball bounced and hit the toe of her shoe. She kicked it back to him.

"Thanks, lady," he said.

"I can't come and get you. This isn't a taxi service," the line clicked and went dead on the other end.

Anson was her last hope, to get back. She'd lose herself and everything she was thinking about. One hit and it would be gone – every thought – every emotion – even if only for a little while.

"You get down here!" her mother shouted. "You dirty little slut!"

It was years ago, but it played in her mind like it was happening now. She could even smell the smell of her mother, a combination of talcum powder and Jack Daniels.

Her sister had been more of a mother to her than her mother had been. Their father had flown the coop, right after she came into the world and her mother always blamed her for his departure.

"You drove him off!" she'd scream.

And her mother would bring men home. Men who'd help her pay the rent, put food on the table. Men who were monsters. Monsters who her mother should have protected her daughter from.

She sighed. Years of therapy had allowed her to forgive her mother. To accept she'd done the best she could have done, under the circumstances.

There it was: The Viaduct.

She shivered, it was remarkably high up – but yes, the homeless man had said the view from up there must be worth the climb. But the shoes on her feet were pinching her, and halfway up, tired of carrying them, she tossed them into Lake Ontario. She laughed thinking about a turtle or fish watching them as they dropped into the bottom of the lake.

Once she got to the top, the view took her breath away. She could see ugliness, buildings which used to have a function. Now they were people-less and uncared for with weeds growing up their walls. There was a naked beauty, one which if she weren't so high up, she would have been able to appreciate.

And in the other direction, Lake Ontario. She followed the path of the water. To the right, one of her shoes popped up and a few moments later the other joined it. They floated along like a ghost was dancing instead of walking on water.

She laughed, first quietly, then hysterically. Her dress billowed around her like she was inside of a cloud.

She stepped out onto the ledge. She was a bad mother, worse than her mother had been. Her mother at least stayed and kept her daughters close. She left the judging to god, or Jesus or whoever.

Katie's biological mother felt like she was not worth saving. She could not be forgiven. She couldn't even forgive herself.

She raked her fake fingernails along her arms. Tracing the tracks left from the needles she had used for such a long time. She felt them now with her fingers. Even if she kicked the habit, they would recognize her vulnerabilities and start begging to be fed.

She moved closer to the edge. Closed her eyes. Smelled the flowers. Listened to the seagulls' cries. Then dropped into the cool waters of Lake Ontario like a puppet whose strings had been cut.

***

When they found her not far from the Viaduct, she'd been in the water for less than twenty-four-hours. Her eyes were wide open, like she was still pondering something somewhere just out of her reach.

Katie's biological mother was waiting to be identified down at the morgue.

CHAPTER THIRTY-FOUR

EL, ABE AND THE LITTLE ONE

"Come back to bed," Abe said, as El gathered her things to take to Katie's room. She kissed him on the forehead, "Would you like a cup of cocoa?"

"You're reading my mind."

"You stay here, under the covers and keep warm. I'll even toss in a few biscuits."

"Thanks, love." He listened as El meandered about in the kitchen, humming as she went. He understood his wife's need to comfort the child, but he too needed comforting. Besides, he worried she was becoming too attached. Why, in a day or two Katie's mother could return. They'd never see her again. Then what?

El returned with the tray. She kissed him on the forehead on the way out.

Katie was sitting up, waiting for El. "I want to go home," she said rubbing her eyes.

"Don't you like it here?" El asked already knowing the answer.

"Of course."

Abe poked his head in, "Who is crying?" El tried to shoo him away. "What can I do to help you, little one?"

"I want to go home and get something."

"Well now," he said, sitting on the end of the bed. "First of all, El and I don't have a key to your house, nor does Benjamin."

"I can get in, through a window. You'd have to lift me up - I did it once when Mommy forgot her key."

"What is it you need?" El asked.

"I don't think you should go," Abe replied.

"I'd like to get my stuffy."

But you have your beautiful doll, little one," El said.

"Oh, she's nice but I've had my stuffy bear since forever and he'll be all alone."

"Let me think on it," Abe said. "Now hush and go to sleep, or El will have to return to her own room."

Without a word Katie snuggled in under the covers and closed her eyes. Abe winked at El and closed the door on the way out

CHPTER THIRTY-FIVE

ABE AND BENJAMIN

Abe took the tray into the kitchen and tidied up, then went into the living room. Benjamin was asleep on the sofa with the television buzzing in the background. He turned it off, then tossed a duvet over the teenager.

Abe returned to his room and fell asleep. The sound of pots and pans in the kitchen and the smell of breakfast cooking made him hungry. He glanced at the clock radio – it was already 9:30! He put on his housecoat and went to the kitchen.

"You should have woken me!" he exclaimed.

Katie jumped.

"I'm sorry," he said. "I meant to say good morning, first."

El nodded, Katie smiled. He backed his way out of the kitchen into the living room, where Benjamin was watching television.

"Did you sleep well?" Abe inquired.

Benjamin didn't speak, instead he turned the volume up on the television to hear what the reporter was saying on the news.

"A woman's body washed up on the shores of Lake Ontario this morning."

The hairs on Benjamin's arms stood up. "God, I hope that's not Katie's Mom."

Outside their front door the newspaper hit the stoop. Abe picked it up, seeing a photo of Katie and Jennifer

Walker on the front page under the heading, "Missing Mother and Daughter." He rolled the newspaper up and tossed it into the bin.

"Come and get it," El called, and they all sat down for breakfast together.

CHAPTER THIRTY-SIX

SGT. MILLER

A meeting down at the station was scheduled with the RCMP. They'd been called in once Wheeler was identified. He'd need to put them in the picture in regard to Katie's whereabouts. They'd keep the information under wraps.

Meanwhile, a new body had washed up on the shores of Lake Ontario. Apparently with tracks up and down her arms.

Before the RCMP arrived, Miller called Abe, to see how Katie was doing.

"She's been having nightmares. She broke a window, hurt herself a little. El managed it all and the child wasn't seriously injured."

"Oh, I'm sorry to hear that," Miller said. "It's difficult for a child to sleep in a strange bed, in a strange home."

"Right now, all she wants is to go home. She misses something she calls her stuffy bear.'

"Sorry Abe, it's out of the question."

"But she can't sleep."

Miller raised his voice; he closed his door. "Abe, you are not to go there under any circumstances. What if a reporter saw you and followed you home?"

"I hear you."

"Keep a low profile, all of you. I'll be in touch and don't forget, we have an unsolved murder. And we don't know where Katie's mother is." He hesitated. "Katie might be our only lead. And I know it seems like a long shot, but children are perceptive. Sometimes they hone-in on things, things which might help us find her mother, save her mother, before it's too late."

"So, you think Mrs. Walker must have been involved with the drug scene since she and Wheeler were, uh, dating?"

"At this stage, I don't know the answer but there's no sign of break and entry."

"Katie told Benjamin, it was Wheeler, who gave her an expensive doll, so, he'd been to the house on more than one occasion. The other ironic part is, he may have purchased the doll from us."

"Really? Did you have a look at your books, see if there's any record of an order? It might be a lead. It might be something."

"I didn't, and you know what, until now when I told you I hadn't even thought about checking my books. Not to mention, since the doll is a replica of the child, one of us here, if he did order from us must've seen a photo of Katie. I don't recall seeing it, but you know, memory – and getting old. It's one of the first things to go." Abe laughed.

Miller said, "Yeah, I understand, but please check and let me know what you find. Anything. Method of payment. Date it was ordered."

"We only offer those dolls in the lead up to Christmas, so it should be easy enough to track down if he did order it from us."

"See if you can find out any other information from Katie. Any ideas about where her mother might have gone. Holiday destinations. Relatives. Friends. Anything at all."

"Would it be better if you sent someone out? An expert at questioning kids?" Abe asked. "Also, since you are sending someone over, why not send them to pick up the stuffy?"

"I'll have to discuss it with my superiors. Could be, as a next step. For now, she knows you and Benjamin and El. Watch her, without letting her know. Ask her questions if she allows it, without eroding the trust she has in you. Right now, you're all she has. She may have witnessed something which could put all of you in danger."

"Like I said, she's been having nightmares."

"Right. Trauma could cause nightmares, sleepwalking. Staying in an unfamiliar environment is an adjustment under normal circumstances. These are far from normal." Miller hesitated. "Come to think of it, I will ask one of my officers to drop by with a DNA kit. The Officer will collect a simple swab of Katie's saliva. If she wants to talk about anything. I mean to someone outside of your home, then, my Officer will give her the opportunity."

"What a clever idea and thanks for letting me know," Abe said. "I think when the child was left alone in the park, she may have suffered abandonment. It shouldn't cause any permanent damage though, should it?"

"Depends on her disposition, I can't say Abe. It would be helpful for you to check for any information you might have in your files."

"Will do."

"I'll be in touch."

"Thanks."

CHAPTER THIRTY-SEVEN

LOST AND FOUND

It was a sunny afternoon, not a cloud in the sky – the perfect day for fishing.

James and Andrea Richards were out on Lake Ontario in their boat, when she noticed something floating on the water. She pulled out a pair of binoculars and had a closer look. It bounced and moved about, but looked like a woman's handbag.

"I swear to God, there a handbag out there," she said to her husband, handing him the binoculars. "Maybe someone was murdered right here on the lake." She shivered although she was warm and wrapped her arms around herself.

James had a look. "You've been reading way too many Agatha Christie novels."

She scoffed.

"But let's go out and have a closer look anyway to give you peace of mind. After all the fish aren't biting today."

"Thanks love," she said.

James pointed the boat in the direction of the floating object and minutes later his wife put the fishing net to use by gathering up a handbag. As she lifted it out of the net, she noticed it was still closed. Wondering if the contents were dry, she opened it up.

"Wait!" he exclaimed.

Too late, as she pulled out the wallet. Everything inside was dry. Although now she thought about it, she realized she'd gone against everything she knew from television and books by disturbing the contents.

Never mind, it was already done. She flipped the wallet open, finding a driver's license, some credit cards, a photo of a baby, a tube of toothpaste and toothbrush (travel size), a phone with a dead battery and some nail glue.

"I think we better call the police," she said.

"Any cash?" James asked.

"No cash," she said as she dialed 911.

After telling the police what they found, they were told an officer would meet them at the shore. The couple drifted for a few moments in silence, while the seagulls screamed over their heads and nabbed the fish which were jumping all around them.

"Sure, now they're hungry!" James said, as he started up the engine and headed in.

CHAPTER THIRTY-EIGHT

MORGUE

Later, after receiving a call from Patterson, Miller went over to the morgue.

"We've confirmed the Jane Doe is no more than twenty-four, and long-term heavy drug user. With tracks like that, she's been an addict for a long time. She's also Primiparous."

"How old would the child be, if it had lived?"

"Seven, maybe eight."

"The age fits," Miller said. "Anything out of the ordinary in your findings?"

"Her drug of choice was cocaine. At the time of her death, she hadn't used in the past twenty-four hours. She was a heavy user – large metabolic buildup of benzoylecgonine over time, but nothing recent."

"Think she was trying to kick the habit?"

"Highly unlikely unless she was booked into a top rehab."

"Such a waste. I'd best get to the office. Let me know if you find anything else," Miller said, making his way toward the door.

"Will do."

Miller's phone rang out.

"Whereabouts?" he asked. "Right. I can fetch it myself. No problem. I'm on the way. I'll head on in as soon as I've got it. Thanks."

Miller met with the Richards' who handed over the bag.

"What happens if no one claims it?" Andrea asked.

"We'll keep it as evidence until someone does," Miller said. "Thank you for handing it in."

CHAPTER THIRTY-NINE

BENJAMIN AND ABE

Miller texted Abe, telling him the name of the Officer who would come to see Katie and take a sample of her DNA. Abe called home and filled Benjamin in on the details.

"Her name is Officer Lane and she'll be arriving any time now."

"No sign of her yet," Benjamin said.

"When she arrives, ask El to give her a cup of tea and wait for me to get there." In the background he heard the doorbell ring.

"Too late, she's already here and El is busy with customers."

"Tell her to close the shop and come in immediately."

"Okay."

"Over and out," Abe said.

Benjamin texted El to close the shop and come to the house immediately. He opened the door.

"My name is Officer Lane," she said.

El arrived asking, "What's the emergency?"

Benjamin extended his hand.

"I'm here to see Katie," Lane said. "And to get a DNA sample."

El extended her hand. She invited Officer Lane into the living area.

"This is Officer Lane, Katie."

"Katie, you can call me Lacey. I have someone here who says he's been missing you." She pulled out a ragged teddy bear.

The child's eyes lit up, as she accepted her stuffy. "Edward," she cried. Then to Officer Lacey she said, "Oh thank you." To the bear she said, "I've missed you so much." She held his face to her ear and said, "Yes." Followed by, "Really?"

Officer Lane smiled. "Edward's a nice name. I'm glad to see you two reunited. Now I'd like to talk to you, about helping us to find your mommy."

"Is she lost?" Katie asked with a pout.

"We're not sure," Lacey said, "but we could sure use your help."

"What do you need me to do?"

Officer Lane reached into her bag and pulled out the DNA kit. She took out a cue tip and opened a container to put it inside. "I'd like to put this in your mouth and take what we call a swab."

"I've only heard of using those in ears," Katie laughed.

"Exactly what my little girl would say," Lane said with a smile.

"What's her name?"

"Her name is Jemma, but we call her Jem."

"What a pretty name, like a jewel," Katie beamed.

The officer smiled. "It's soft so won't hurt. I'll run it inside your mouth, then put it into this container and we'll send it to a lab."

"If you're scared Katie," Benjamin said, "Officer Lane you can swab me first, so you can see what it's like."

"I'm not scared," Katie said.

The officer took the sample, then wrote Katie's name on the label. She applied it to the container. "When is your birthday? And how old are you?"

"It's September 1, and I'm seven and a half."

After the Officer completed the test, she asked the others if she could have a chat with Katie on her own.

"You don't have to," Benjamin said. "If you don't want to."

"He's right Katie. You don't have to," Lane said. "You want to help us, to find your mother, don't you? I mean if you could help, you'd want to, wouldn't you?"

Katie looked at El.

"What a thing to ask," El said. "Of course, she wants to help, but she's only a child."

Katie nodded to Officer Lane and led her into her room, where she showed her her doll, and began talking about it.

"Mark, Mr. Wheeler bought this doll for me, for Christmas, as a surprise. He was always coming over and bringing me surprises."

"Was he nice?"

"Yes," Katie said.

"Anything else you want to tell me?"

"He and my mommy were happy sometimes." She looked away. "Other times they'd yell, and he would leave."

"Did your mommy cry? When he went?"

"Yes, until we went out for milkshakes."

"You like milkshakes?"

"Yes, strawberry is my favourite."

"Then what would happen?" Lane inquired.

"He'd send presents to my mommy and sometimes to me."

"Very kind of him," Lane said, playing with the hair of the doll and then Katie's hair.

"They don't feel the same," Katie said. "Mine is softer."

"You're right."

"It's because El uses a special conditioner on my hair and she brushes it fifty strokes every night before I go to sleep. She said adults get one hundred strokes and children get fifty strokes." Katie giggled.

Officer Lane looked at the taped-up window, "What happened here?"

"El said I was sleepwalking. I don't remember."

"Did you ever sleepwalk before?"

"I don't think so," Katie replied. "El put bandages on me. She's a trained nurse. My mommy wanted to be a teacher, but..."

"What stopped her?"

"Me, being born," Katie said. She put her doll back onto the bed and asked, "Is there anything else? To help find my mommy?"

"I wondered, if you have any aunts or uncles, grandparents, friends, who your mom might have gone to stay with? What about your dad?"

"Mommy has a sister, but I never met her. Mommy's older. I never met my grandparents. I never met my dad."

"Where does your mother's sister live? So, we could call her?"

"I don't know."

"Have you ever lived anywhere else?" Lacey asked.

"No." Katie looked at her feet. "Sorry I'm not much help."

Officer Lane patted her on the head, "I don't know, sometimes we know more than we think we know. Keep thinking."

"Thanks again for my stuffy."

"My pleasure."

Officer Lane made her way to the lab with the sample and put it on the high priority list. After a short conversation, she was able to push it to the top. She made her way back to the station.

***

Miller received a call from Officer Lane.

"As requested, I took Katie Walker's DNA sample straight down to the lab. They did a comparison with the woman down at the morgue – they're a match."

"I'm not looking forward to sharing this news. It's the worst outcome."

"If you need me, I'll go along with you for support."

"Thanks for the offer, but this is a time when our on-staff counsellor will be extremely useful. We haven't had cause to use her often since she works off-site. I haven't had much contact with Counsellor Briggs, have you?"

"Haven't even met the woman," Officer Lane said.

"Guess I'll be the first to work with her from our station."

"Whatever happens Sarge, she should be well trained to handle it."

"I sure hope so. Thanks, and see you back at the station." He disconnected realizing he didn't have Eleanor Briggs' number in his phone. He called the station again and asked the Front Desk Officer to locate the number. He entered the info into his phone and gave Briggs a call and filled her in on the situation.

"I can be ready as soon as you need me," Briggs indicated.

"Okay, I'll swing by and get you in about fifteen minutes," Miller said, making a u-turn. He couldn't stop himself from thinking about Katie. This news would break her heart.

Reluctantly he dialed Abe's number and filled him in on the situation.

Benjamin was feeling claustrophobic and wished the shop could open. It would be a welcome distraction. He texted Abe, "Where r u?"

Abe was nearly home when he received the text, then a call from Sgt. Miller came through.

"I have sad news about Katie's mother. Her body was found near the Viaduct."

"Suicide?"

"It hasn't been ruled out."

"Okay. Incredibly sad news indeed. Poor Katie. Should I tell her, now? I'm just heading inside."

"No. A counsellor and I are coming over to tell Katie. Will you, Benjamin and El be present? She'll need your support."

"Uh, yes. Such a sad outcome. Of course, we'll all be there."

Arriving home, he went into the family room and saw Katie snuggled up to a stuffed toy. "Who's this now?" he asked.

"It's Edward Bear, my stuffy."

"I'd like to take a closer look, if you can run into my room and bring me my glasses."

Katie scampered out and down the hall. He waved Benjamin and El closer and told them the sad news.

***

"Poor Katie," El said, with tears in her eyes.

Benjamin said nothing.

"Sgt. Miller is coming over with a counsellor to tell Katie. They would like us to be here to support her. The counsellor will manage the situation, she's trained to help children in traumatic situations."

"Katie will be heart-broken, the poor darling. Whatever will become of her?"

"And after they tell her, then what?" Benjamin said, his shoulders slumped. He body collapsed in on itself, like he'd just taken a punch in the gut. "Are they going to take her away, send her to live with foster parents – I mean, with strangers?"

"She is happy here," El said.

"Except for the window incident and the nightmares," Abe said.

"It will be out of our hands, after she knows her mother is gone. She may have relatives," El said.

"If not, she'll go into the foster care system. She can't go into the system," Benjamin said.

"She has been with us for a few days, Sgt. Miller will ensure that Katie is the priority, and he knows us."

"We love Katie," El said.

Katie arrived in the room with Abe's glasses. He bent down so she could put them onto his face.

"Thank you, little one," he said, as he patted her on the head.

Abe, El and Benjamin formed a circle with Katie in the middle. They lifted her up and spun her around and around. She giggled, threw her head back and imagined she was flying.

CHAPTER FORTY

BAD NEWS

A knock on the door interrupted their jolliness. They put Katie down onto the floor then Benjamin and El stood behind her. Each had a hand on her shoulder. Abe went to answer the door and returned moments later with Sgt. Miller and the counsellor.

Benjamin tightened his grip on Katie's shoulder.

"You all know me," Sgt. Miller said. "Except for you Katie, I'm an old friend of the Julius.' And this is Counsellor Briggs. She works with me down at the police station."

Abe shook Briggs' manly hand, while Katie, El and Benjamin remained where they were.

"You have a lovely home," Briggs said in the direction of El.

Briggs was nearly as tall as Miller and with shoulders like that, she looked like she could have played linebacker for the Packers. Her strawberry hair looked like she stuck her finger in a socket then applied hairspray. And her face, rather than being round or oval was made square by her bangs, hair, and lack of neck. Her nose was off centre, so one was never sure if her cross-eyed green eyes were looking at it, or at whoever she was speaking to. Briggs advanced toward Katie who hid behind Benjamin and El.

Miller said, "Katie, Counsellor Briggs, Eleanor, would like to tell you something. It's important."

Katie remained where she was until Benjamin and El took her hands.

"I will tell her," El said, as she and Benjamin led her toward the chair. When they were face to face, El said, "Katie darling, your mommy has gone to heaven."

Briggs intervened. "Your mother has died, Katie."

El took Katie into her arms.

"Katie," Briggs said, bending down to touch her on the back. "Understand? About your mother? Anything you'd like to ask me? It's all right If you'd like to cry."

Katie saying nothing, moved across the room, where she stretched out her arms and began to turn. She looked like she was pretending to be a windmill.

"She's not dead," she sang to an all too familiar tune – Frere Jacques.

Benjamin with tears streaming down his cheeks scooped her up into his arms.

All the while Katie screamed, "She's not dead! She's not dead!" while pounding her tiny, clenched fists against his chest.

Benjamin let her hit out all the pain using him as her punching bag. When she was empty of all emotion and exhausted, she went limp in his arms like a ragdoll. He carried her to her room, tucked her into bed. She closed her eyes. Tears seeped through every now and then, he wiped them away and holding her hand watched her drift off to sleep.

In the hallway, Briggs turned to El, "Katie is a ward of the court now. They will decide what is best for her."

"She just lost her mom," El said, clenching her fists so tightly that her nails broke through the skin. "What kind of woman are you?"

"Whoa. She's only doing her job El," Sgt. Miller said.

"You'll need a court order, to remove her from my home," Abe said.

Sgt. Miller glared at his old friend. "Hold on now Abe. We have no intention of storming her room and tearing her out of her bed. She's only just lost her mother and we wouldn't do it to her or any child, not now, or ever.

Besides, she knows you and she's better off in a familiar place with people she trusts and knows."

"She's a part of our family now," El said.

"Yes, but she's not your child," Briggs said. "Besides, there are laws and protocols which must be followed."

"You are a cold woman," El said getting all up in Briggs' face.

Miller pulled them apart. "I'll have a word with her," he said to El. Then to Briggs, "We can talk about this outside."

Briggs put her hands on her hips. "Sure, we can continue this discussion outside."

She took a step toward the door, then said to El and Abe, "So, you are aware of the procedure. Once I get the paperwork filed, a judge will decide what the next step will be. Normal procedure is for the child be handed over. Usually within the next twenty-four to forty-eight-hour period. Failure to do so, will result in a fine for obstruction, endangerment and possibly even jail time. It all depends on the judge assigned to Katie's case." She turned her back on them and headed for the exit.

"Her name is Katie," El called after her.

Miller apologized profusely as he followed Briggs out the door.

CHAPTER FORTY-ONE

MILLER AND BRIGGS

Miller clicked the door of his cruiser open. Once inside he slammed it shut. After taking a couple of deep breaths he unlocked the passenger door to let Briggs into the vehicle. As she fastened her seatbelt, he crashed his clenched fists down on the steering wheel. "You didn't have to be so hard on them."

"They have become too attached, to a child who is not theirs. A child who belongs with family, not incidental strangers. She needs more than ever to be with blood relatives, not wannabe relatives."

"What if there are no blood relatives?"

Briggs shook her head. "Unless we look, we'll never know. It is our duty to the child, to seek them out. To leave no stone unturned. To ensure she receives the best of care with people who will help her to manage her grief."

"They love her, have made her a part of their family and I've known them for years."

"I know you have, but there's something. Something isn't right. I can't put my finger on it, but it's there."

As he backed out of the driveway, Miller took in another deep breath. "But if it weren't for them, she might have been abducted or murdered. They saved her, rescued her. God knows what would have happened to her if she'd been left alone at the waterfront all night. You know what the area is like after dark. Druggies and prostitutes. The child was damned lucky the Julius' family found her, took her in and treated her like she was their own child."

"I understand where you're coming from Sgt. Miller, but even you must realize the child has to be the priority here. And I have to follow my instincts."

He was so angry he couldn't speak, so instead he dug his nails into the leather steering wheel protector while she continued waffling on.

"You've been in the force for years now, and your reputation is outstanding. And yet, you are letting your own emotions play on you. From what I hear, you allowed the force to foot the bill, searching for a child who you knew the whereabouts of for days? You even pretended to the press we were still looking for not just her mother, but for Katie too. As you very well know, on both accounts your actions were against procedures."

Miller dug his fingernails further into the steering wheel protector. He held his breath and concentrated on the road. If he did not, he would become extremely angry and...he didn't want to lose control when she was flipping his switch. Trying to make him lose his cool by questioning his integrity. He was her superior, in every way and yet, here she was droning on like...

"Oh, I get it," she said. "They are your friends, and they can't have a kid so hey, presto, here's everyone's child no one wants."

Miller slammed on the brakes as the light went from amber to red. "Who do you think you are talking to?" he demanded. "In the first place, no one as you call it, "foot the bill." In fact, I followed protocol, and reported to the D.P.C. about Katie staying with Abe and his wife. He told me to monitor the situation which I did. And when the RCMP became involved, I let them know where she was. I follow protocol."

She shook her head, "I'm sorry, this isn't personal. It's why the system exists, to protect those who cannot protect themselves."

He acknowledged her last statement with a nod, knowing it to be true. Leaving Katie where she was made sense, but Briggs was right about one thing, rules were rules. The facts were thus: the couple was elderly, and this could sway the courts.

"This is my jurisdiction," Miller said. "Don't flaunt the rulebook at me. I was following the rules, while you were still being pushed around in a pram."

Briggs laughed.

He continued, now calmer. "The system has its flaws, the child, Katie did not get lost in the system. She was given over to the care of The Julius' family who are pillars in our community."

Briggs was quiet for a bit. "Given is the word I object to. A child isn't a puppy to be handed over. A judge must look at the facts and decide this case. The judge will see things in black and white. They will not be influenced by emotions."

"I'd vouch for Abe and El. Hell, if I died, I couldn't think of a better couple to look after my own kids – that is if they were still kids. Mine have all grown up."

"This isn't about you, Sgt. Miller. This isn't your fight."

Miller was silent. She was right about another thing: it wasn't his fight. Still, he knew Abe and his family.

Miller dropped Briggs off at her parked car and headed to the station. She made him so angry, furious. What he hated the most was how right she was. On one hand, most judges wouldn't care about Abe and El and how old they were.

On the other hand, they wouldn't give a hoot about counsellor Briggs' so-called instincts. Especially not if he got in there and plead the Julius' case first. He figured it would take Briggs at least thirty minutes to get back to the office. Give or take depending upon traffic. In the meantime, he'd set a plan to action.

Back in the office, Miller clicked onto the database and read Officer Lane's report. He typed in an updated addendum:

Date, Time. Sgt. Alex Miller and Counsellor Eleanor Briggs met at the house of the Julius' Family, where Katie Walker has been staying since her mother disappeared on

Date, Time. With Abe, his wife, El and their foster son – he typed over foster – added adopted.

He stopped, being unsure whether the boy was still being fostered or adopted. He retyped foster son, while Katie was informed of her mother's death.

In my opinion, the child should remain with the Julius' family. She knows them and has built up trust. Relocating her, in this time of grief, to unfamiliar surroundings, with people she doesn't know would be a cruel and unnecessary change and it could have repercussions on the little girl's chance of surviving the loss of her mother.

He stopped typing and re-read. He felt the need to address Briggs' intuition. The truth was the only person who'd upset the child was Briggs herself.

He clicked the file closed.

Miller made a phone call to a judge friend of his, Judge Anders who suggested a preliminary hearing be set. Anders agreed there was no reason to uproot the child.

"Ask the petitioner to come to the courthouse in one hour's time," Anders said. "And we can put things in motion."

"Thank you," Miller replied. He hung up and called Abe and explained the urgency of his coming to the courthouse. "Meet me in the entry way, as quick as you can. We'll see Judge Anders' in his Chambers together and sort out the paperwork." He hesitated then continued. "I've called in a favour which I hope will be enough to allow you to keep Katie with you," Miller said. "So, don't be late."

"On the way," Abe said, and he ordered a taxi. The minute he got inside the vehicle, even before he had a chance to buckle up his seatbelt, he instructed the driver to get him to the courthouse a.s.a.p.

"If I get a ticket, you must pay the bill," the driver said.

"I'm not telling you to break the law, just step on it and avoid the most congested routes."

"Sure thing," the driver replied.

***

Now back in her office, Eleanor Briggs scrolled through the child named Katie Walker's files on-line. Bingo, she found a recent report written by Officer Lacey Lane. In it, Lane said Katie was having nightmares and sleepwalking. On one occasion she even self-harmed. El Julius tended to her without calling an ambulance claiming to be a qualified nurse.

To the original document she typed in the following addendum:

Date, Time. Counsellor Eleanor Briggs and Sgt. Alex Miller attended the Julius' home where Katie Walker, was informed of her mother's death. Also, in attendance were Abe, El and Benjamin Julius.

Katie had been staying with them since her mother's disappearance on Date. The child received the news as well as could be received under the circumstances.

However, El Julius became hostile when Briggs attempted to communicate with the child directly. After reading Officer's Lane's report it is this Counsellor's opinion said nightmares could have been the direct result of Mrs. Julius' over mothering. This is a troubling, as Katie's mother, until today – was deemed to be alive. It is therefore my recommendation for Katie Walker be removed from the Julius' home immediately. Preferably to be relocated to a home with a blood relative.

She stopped typing and pondered for a moment. Did reading this information, shed any light on the gut feeling she had? She decided it did not. Still, now she had more information which would make her case stronger.

Briggs was certain most judges would follow her recommendations and take little Katie Walker into provincial care.

She pushed SEND.

CHAPTER FORTY-TWO

BRIGGS MISSES IT

A friend who worked in Judge Anders' office owed Eleanor Briggs a favour. She called and filled her in on the situation. "Son of a bitch," Briggs exclaimed. Anders was not the kind of judge you could ring up and negotiate with. Face to face was the only way with him. She ran out of the building, down to her car and made her way to the courthouse.

Briggs could not believe Miller would reach out to a judge, let alone one who she never saw eye-to-eye with. Although, upon consideration she did not think Miller would know they'd butted heads. Then again, word got around in the precinct. People talked. Gossiped like in any other career. It was too much of a coincidence.

Miller had to have known. She swerved around a corner, squealing her tires as the light turned yellow.

She thumped her fists down on the steering wheel. She still could not believe it was Judge Anders who was sitting this preliminary hearing. He was well-known for his leniency and loved stories which pulled at his heartstrings. He was a good, fair, and just judge, but he wore his heart on his sleeve – some thought it was his best quality as a judge. For Briggs following rules by the book was the only way to work. If only Anders knew about the nightmares and Mrs. Julius' pretending to be a nurse – it could change everything.

Briggs made it to the judge's chambers, just as Miller and Abe were exiting.

"You're too late," Miller said. "Judge Anders has approved our request for Katie to remain with the Julius' for one month's time. He will revisit the case when the term ends."

Briggs pushed her way through the two men and entered Anders' Chambers and closed the door behind her.

"He is not going to appreciate being second guessed," Miller said as he and Abe left the building.

CHAPTER FORTY-THREE

ABE AND MILLER

Miller was pleased with the outcome as he drove Abe home. The only thing which could change things for Katie in the next month, would be if a relative came forward. Otherwise, the child would remain in their care indefinitely.

Abe was quiet until the car stopped at his house. "What happens if, Briggs gets her way and Katie is sent to live with total and complete strangers?"

"We won a ruling in our favour, let's not worry about it now."

"But I worry. I'm certain Benjamin and El will be concerned too. Should we tell the child she may only be with us for a month? To prepare her?"

"A month to a little girl like Katie is a long time," Miller said. "And she's still grieving for her mother."

"It will be a difficult road ahead, but thank you," Abe said getting out of the car. He waved as Sgt. Miller pulled away.

CHAPTER FORTY-FOUR

KATIE

When Katie awoke, she was staring up at the ceiling. The tiny rose petals looked even prettier today with the sun shining in on them. She watched the red petals, dancing in mid-air, rolling and flitting like in a movie.

El was sound asleep beside her and Benjamin was sleeping on the chair. She remembered something wonderful had happened and then something not so wonderful.

She closed her eyes and tried to remember both the good and the bad. She thought about the man in the police uniform and the scary woman. She flinched remembering the woman had grabbed her.

Then she remembered. The bad woman said her mommy was dead, but she wasn't. She wailed.

Benjamin and El enclosed the child in their arms.

"She's not dead," she said with teary eyes.

"It is going to be okay," El said, fighting back the tears.

"We're right here for you," Benjamin soothed.

Benjamin knew he could not take away her pain, it was hers and hers alone. He had experienced the same pain of loss himself. It is how he knew he could help her by sharing in her pain, like Abe had done for him a long, long, ago. Then he had poured his pain into Abe, now he would allow Katie to pour her pain into him.

CHAPTER FORTY-FIVE

MORE KATIE

When Abe went inside, he found Benjamin and El in Katie's room.

"I need to speak with you, El," he whispered.

She came out, leaving Benjamin and Katie behind with the door ajar.

Abe took his wife by the hand and led her down the hall.

"Are they taking her away from us?" she asked.

"Come along into the kitchen when we can talk properly."

Benjamin had woken up had been listening in, until they moved away into the kitchen.

"No, we had a win today, she can remain with us for at least another month, and possibly indefinitely."

"I'm glad she doesn't have to be relocated. She is in no shape to be taken away to live with strangers. I couldn't bear it."

"It's only temporary, but thanks to Sgt. Miller's advocacy, it is a win."

"We need to tell Benjamin."

They went to Katie's room. She was sleeping, Benjamin on the other hand, was nowhere to be found. Returning to Katie's room, El caressed the little girl's head. She threw back the covers: it was the doll, not Katie. "Oh no!" she exclaimed.

The elderly couple searched in every room in the house, then they went into the garden. Still no sign of either Katie or Benjamin.

"Where could they have gone?" El asked.

"I don't know," Abe said.

"She was so distraught. We'd only settled her down before you asked to speak with me." She gasped. "Maybe Benjamin thought they would take her away and so, he took her before they could. When you called me out of the room...He must've thought." She wept into her hands.

"They can't have gone far."

CHAPTER FORTY-SIX

BENJAMIN AND KATIE

He carried the sleeping child in his arms and got into the taxi he'd ordered.

"My sister fell asleep, before I could take her home," he explained.

The driver shrugged.

Benjamin stroked Katie's hair as she slept. Taking her, had been the only way to keep her safe. There were dangers all around. Dangers which only he could protect her from.

Forty-five minutes later, on the other side of town. "You can drop us off here," Benjamin said.

"She sure is a sound sleeper," the driver said. He got out and opened the door. Benjamin placed a few bills into his hand.

The man at the door opened it, and he collected the key. In the elevator, Katie stirred for a moment, then went back to sleep again.

Arriving on the seventh floor, he opened the door and carefully put her down onto the bed. He closed the drapes, put a blanket over her and sat in a chair near the bed. He dozed off.

"What happened? Where am I?" Katie asked, rubbing her eyes, and trying to get out of bed. Unable to do so, she remained on the pillow. A few hours had passed, and she was in an unfamiliar place. A place which smelled like candy floss and burned toast.

Benjamin had waited for Katie to come to before he spoke to her. As the drugs he'd given her had worn-off he could talk to her. Explain things. Keep her calm.

He did not want her to scream. Someone might hear her if she screamed. Then he would have to hurt her. He did not want to hurt her.

CHAPTER FORTY-SEVEN

ABE AND EL

"I think we better ring Sgt. Miller and let him know," Abe said.

El stopped him. "Why? Everything will be fine. He will bring her back. She won't have gone far, not without her doll."

"I have a bad feeling about this," Abe said. "I'm ringing Sgt. Miller." He got up and went to the phone. Picked it up and began dialing.

"You're right, Abe." She moved closer to him just as her husband put the phone down and turned her back to walk away. "We must be the ones to report it. Both children are missing."

She followed closely on her husband's heels. "It's our responsibility. We need to find the children, and quickly."

"And we will, there's no need for panic."

"Perhaps," El said, while Abe once again put down the phone receiver. "Perhaps. But..." El walked toward the front door. "I'm going outside, to call for them. Maybe they're hiding. Having a game of hide and seek."

Abe caught her by the arm. Pulled her back inside, into the living room.

El watched in silence as her husband paced and grew more agitated with every passing moment.

CHAPTER FORTY-EIGHT

KATIE

On a chair beside the bed sat Benjamin. He looked like Benjamin and then he didn't. He was all blurry and far away.

Where was El? Where was Abe?

She looked up at the ceiling, there were no dancing rose petals in this room. The room began to spin, as her stomach rose to her throat.

Benjamin was at her side, holding an ice bucket in which she vomited. When she finished, he went into the bathroom and flushed the contents of the bucket down the toilet. He ran cool water on a washcloth and went back to place it upon the child's forehead.

"Better now?" he asked as his phone vibrated. Abe was calling. He turned his phone off, removed the battery. Put it on the ground and stomped on it, then tossed the remains into the bin.

Katie watched silently until he returned. "Yes, thank you," she said. He sat on the end of the bed, looking at her. "Where are we? Where is my mommy? I want my mommy! And where are Abe and El? I want El."

Benjamin turned away and stood. "They had to go away. Like your mommy had to go away." He moved across the room and dropped into a chair. He pulled his legs up, so he was sitting yoga style, then closed his eyes like he was planning to mediate.

Katie sobbed.

He opened his eyes. "It's you and me now, you and me kid." He closed his eyes again and covered his face.

Katie began wailing, "I want my mommy. I want my mommy!"

Benjamin moved across the floor toward her.

She recoiled from him, wrapping her arms around herself.

CHAPTER FORTY-NINE

EL AND ABE

El was becoming more impatient with Abe's inaction.

"We have to do something, now," she said. "Time is ticking away, and anything could happen. I wish I hadn't stopped you from calling Alex. I wish..."

She reached for the phone.

"Don't," Abe said, grabbing hold of her arm. "Just don't."

CHAPTER FIFTY

A FEELING

Sgt. Miller had a file waiting on his desk when he returned to his office. He flipped through a report confirming the dead woman's name was Margaret (Maggie) Monahan. He stopped and sat back in his chair. Wait. Katie's mother was Jennifer Walker. But the DNA report was a match for Katie.

He leaned forward and continued to read about Margaret Monahan. As his finger ran down her bio, he confirmed a connection: a sister. Margaret Monahan was the married name of Jennifer Walker's sister.

He read on, discovering both parents died before Katie's birth. So, she had never met her grandparents.

He thought about Katie's reaction to the news. How she had adamantly refused to believe it – and she'd been right.

Miller stormed out of his office, needing to go somewhere, but not knowing why yet. Abe's name popped into his head. Why? He called him. No answer. Yet something was nagging at him. He went to his car, hit the siren which parted traffic on all sides as he went to Abe's house.

As he pulled into the driveway, he immediately noticed the front door was standing wide open. The adjacent shop had a CLOSED sign on the window.

Miller went inside, calling out, "Anyone home? It's Alex Miller. Abe? El?"

The house was tidy and quiet. No sound of the television or radio. But something was indeed off, his feeling had been right. He withdrew his weapon, and rounded the corner, leading into the living room.

There was a body on the floor: the body of El Julius.

CHAPTER FIFTY-ONE

ABE

After trying to call Benjamin – no answer – Abe went out into the street and flagged down a taxi.

"Take me to the train station," he demanded, fumbling in his wallet. In his hurry, he'd forgotten to bring extra cash. He'd get it at the station.

"Sure thing," the driver said, then he turned up the radio.

Abe tried to ring Benjamin again without any luck. Would the boy be so idiotic, as to take the child to their secret place?

CHAPTER FIFTY-TWO

KATIE AND BENJAMIN

Benjamin put his arm around Katie's shoulder, and they sat side by side on the bed without speaking. She nuzzled into him.

"Benji," she said, wrapping her arms around his waist.

He kissed her on top of the head. He hummed, a lullaby, until she went back to sleep. He covered his ears. He hated the sound of the mini refrigerator buzzing. He pulled the plug out of the wall.

CHAPTER FIFTY-THREE

MILLER AND EL

"Jesus, El," Miller said, going down on one knee to feel her pulse. It was there, faint, but there. He cradled her head in his arm and she opened her eyes.

"Who did this to you?"

"Abe," she whispered.

Miller leaned in closer, he hadn't heard correctly. Had he?

"Abe. It was Abe," she said, eyes rolling back in her head as with his free hand he typed 911 into his phone.

After the ambulance drove away with siren screaming, Sgt. Miller tried to find Abe, Benjamin, and Katie. Where were they? Had they all gone somewhere together leaving El in this state?

As Miller went over everything, with nothing making an inch of sense his phone rang. He hoped someone knew something. And El was going to be okay. She had to be.

"Sorry, Sarge, but she went into cardiac arrest," the ambulance driver said. "We couldn't save her."

"Oh no," Miller said, disconnecting.

He had to think this through. He had to clear his head. He had to find Katie Walker and tell her she was right. Her mother really wasn't dead, but El was. How was he going to break the news to them?

Miller called the station and asked for a team to be sent down to trace any incoming calls.

"As soon as possible - I mean yesterday," he said.

Moments later a team was on their way to the Julius' house.

CHAPTER FIFTY-FOUR

BENJAMIN AND KATIE

Cradling Katie's head, Benjamin rocked back and forth and back and forth. He pretended they were in a rocking chair, although they weren't in one. Instead, they were in the secret place. The secret place where all the forgotten children went.

The other children were running and playing, while Katie slept on. Benjamin waved to them, then put his fingers to his lips.

"Shhhh," he whispered.

He played with her hair, thinking about how he would explain the decision he'd made. It wasn't the first time he'd taken someone to the secret place: the place inside Van Gogh's Sunflowers painting.

But Katie was the youngest, so he had to choose each word carefully, thoughtfully. He realized when she first woke up, she'd be frightened. It was also why he'd given her more of the sleeping medicine, while he decided what to do. He hoped her transition would be calm and simple. Since she was an orphan now too. They'd be together, with the other children. No one needed to be alone, not here in this new world.

He remembered the first time he woke up in Van Gogh's world. Abe had never guessed he was out of his body while the old man did vile things to it.

And now he'd never know. Because he, Katie and the others were safely hidden in a new world where adults were not permitted to go.

CHAPTER FIFTY-FIVE

ABE

Arriving at the train station, Abe looked at the schedule. He bought a ticket, then synchronized his watch with the estimated time of arrive. He had a while to wait. To wait and to worry. He walked across the platform, sat down on an empty bench, and began going through his worries one by one. This method of tackling each problem had been a valuable strategy for him in the past.

First, he made a mental list starting with El, Benjamin and ending with Katie. It was a brief list; one he could easily get a handle on quickly.

The incident with El was unfortunate. She overreacted, which caused him to do the same. If she would have only let him handle things.

She'd done so in the past thus avoiding a confrontation. He hadn't hit her hard. It was just a love tap. She would recover and forgive all, like she always did. He dialed home to check on her.

"Hello," a voice, a man's voice barked, as Abe made his way to the cash machine. Then having withdrawn some money, checked which platform his train would be arriving on and made his way there.

Abe didn't speak, because he was stunned into silence when he recognized Alex Miller's voice on the other end. What what he doing there? Had El called him? Was she intending to press charges against him? She'd never have done so in the past because they always worked it out between the two of them.

"Abe is that you? El is dead. Abe? Abe?"

Abe could not believe it. El could not be dead. He let go of the phone and it hit the pavement. He heard Alex calling his name, picked up the phone. Thank goodness it still worked.

"She's what? No, she can't be!"

Behind him, Miller's team of officers were tracing Abe's whereabouts, trying to get his phone to synchronize and broadcast his location. The officer used hand signals to indicate they needed more time.

Miller said. "She had a bad knock on the head, I called the ambulance, but she didn't make it to the hospital. Where are the children? Neither Katie nor Benjamin are in the house. Where are you?"

Abe walked toward the stairs, wanting to head home. He needed to stick to the plan. To find Benjamin and Katie.

The officer again indicated Miller should stretch out the call by keeping him on the line.

"Your front door was wide open when I got here. I was worried about you, Abe. We've been friends for so long, I just had a gut feeling. Like you needed me or something," Miller looked over, they were zeroing in on his location.

He continued. "Was just thinking about the time when you and I took my two boys out on the boat and did a little fishing? Remember? Seems like so long ago now, we ought to do it again. We could take Benjamin and Katie this time. They'd love it. Don't you think?"

Abe said. "I can't believe it about El. How can she be dead? Who would ever hurt El?" He stopped, then asked, "Did she, say anything?

"No, Abe, she was unconscious when I arrived. I've been in the force so long, and we've been friends for so long, guess we're connected. Like I said, when I arrived the door was standing wide open."

Abe inhaled.

"Are you okay? Where are you? I'll come and get you; you'll want to see her, and we can find the two kids, they need to know."

A train whistle sounded, followed by a chugging sound.

"I have to go now," Abe said. His old friend was rambling – not something he'd do under normal circumstances. El had said something. Now they were trying to find his location. He tossed his phone into the rubbish bin.

"Wait Abe!" Miller shouted, he looked at the officer.

"We have his location, at a train station on the east side. I just checked and the train on the platform departed, but he's still on the platform."

"Send me the location, I'll head over there now."

"Will do," the officer said.

When he got into his car, he put the flashing light on the roof. He set the sirens blaring, which allowed him to cut through congested traffic like butter.

CHAPTER FIFTY-SIX

ABE AND THE TRAIN

On the train now, Abe sat in a seat away from other passengers so he could think. El was gone. She was dead. He'd killed her, but it was an accident. He hadn't meant to hurt her. His life wasn't worth anything without her in it.

The first stop, he watched passengers on the platform. It was annoying to see them walking around like robots with their full attention on their phones. If anyone walked up behind them, they could shove them onto the tracks. They'd be dead before they knew what happened. Sad what the world had come to. Walking robots.

It was why he had avoided using a cell phone for so long. It wasn't until Benjamin taught him the benefits of having it on hand, so he gave it a go. When they'd meet, at short notice, they'd text each other. Their messages would be in code, so no one else would know what they were talking about. It was exciting, fun.

Thinking about El's death, Abe invented a story in his mind. It was one he would tell Sgt. Miller next time he saw him. He'd start by telling his old friend, how Benjamin, was afraid they were going to take Katie into care. Benjamin who'd been abused in the foster system. How the poor and distraught teenager had accidentally shoved El. El had fallen to the floor. How he, himself had checked and El was lucid, then, with El's okay had run out of the house to find

Benjamin who'd taken Katie after he hurt El and made a run for it.

Yes, after all he'd done for the boy, he'd convince him to go along with the story. He had his ways of convincing the boy to do anything he wanted him to do.

Someone moved into the seat behind him: a woman by the smell of her perfume. He glanced around, yes, a young woman. Perhaps twenty five. On the way to work or to a party, he thought, all dressed up to the nines. He watched her pull an apple out of her bag, and cringed when she took one bite, then several others. She chewed with her mouth open. A bit of apple juice splashed onto his neck. He wiped it away. Disgusting and annoying. She crunched and chewed. Crunched and chewed. He was waiting for the next crunch, waiting with tensed shoulders, but it never came. He glanced back to see why and discovered the woman was choking.

"Anyone know the Heimlich Maneuver?" Abe shouted, but he and the woman were the only ones in the carriage.

He closed, his mouth, realizing his shouting had drawn attention to the situation and for a split second, maybe more, he wished he'd let the woman choke.

As fellow passengers made their way toward them, he thumped the woman hard on the back and she spit the apple onto the floor.

CHAPTER FIFTY-SEVEN

MILLER IN PURSUIT

Miller zipped through traffic. He commanded a spot at the train station entryway. He left his lights flashing so the ticket officers wouldn't book him. He ran up the stairs.

"You're nearly there. Straight ahead. Just to the left of you," the surveillance officer said.

"The only thing on the platform besides me, is a garbage bin," Miller said. He walked toward it.

"Yes, it's where the signal is coming from."

Sgt. Miller put on his gloves and put his hands into the bin. Shoving aside a banana peel, he found what he was looking for: Abe's phone.

"Can I help you?" a conductor asked.

"Yes, how long since the last train left here?"

"Fifteen minutes ago, but they didn't get far."

Miller did a double take. "How so?"

The conductor continued. "The train stopped for an emergency with a passenger on board. The ambulance has collected a woman and she's on the way to the hospital. A victim of an apple getting lodge in her throat. They say she's going to be okay, just checking her out to be certain for insurance purposes."

"What was the train's final destination?" Miller asked.

"It's an Express, so only one stop at the end of the line."

"Thank you," Miller said. He rushed down the stairs, into his vehicle and activated the siren.

CHAPTER FIFTY-EIGHT

ABE THE GOOD SAMARITAN

No longer on the train, Abe held the woman's hand whom he had saved. They were in the back of an ambulance and on the way to the hospital.

Shortly after she spit out the apple, the ambulance arrived. The annoying young woman refused to get into the vehicle, unless Abe went along to the hospital with her.

"He's my Good Samaritan," the woman said.

After the paramedics pushed the woman inside the hospital on a stretcher, Abe saw his chance to escape. He called a taxi. While he was waiting on the platform, the driver of the ambulance came out.

"Thank you for taking control of the situation and saving her life."

"Sure thing," Abe said through the open window. Then to the driver, "Drop me off at the corner of Magnolia and Oak."

The white van pulled away, as the ambulance driver got inside the cab of his vehicle. A message came over the radio, asking all drivers to be on the lookout for a man meeting Abe's description.

CHAPTER FIFTY-NINE

MILLER AND ABE

Miller's phone rang. "An ambulance driver just called. He said a man fitting Abe's description left a few minutes ago in a white van. Yes, from the hospital. He said Abe saved a woman's life on the train."

"Sounds more like the Abe I know. Did the driver manage to get the plate number?"

"No, but he heard the elderly gentleman ask to be taken to the corner of Magnolia and Oak."

"I'm nearly there now," Miller said, disconnecting. He wondered what was in the vicinity – it was a well-known seedy area where hookers lined the streets even in the daytime.

A few blocks later, a white van stopped at the lights near Magnolia. Miller got out of his vehicle and approached the passenger's side. Abe wasn't a spring chicken, but he didn't want to take any chances he might run. No passenger was in the vehicle.

Abe flashed his I.D. then asked if he'd brought a passenger, an older gentleman to this location. The man nodded. "Where did he go?"

"He got out, a couple of blocks back. Paid me with cash then said he'd walk the rest of the way."

"So close," Miller said, as he returned to his vehicle, then he changed his mind and moved onto the sidewalk. He looked up and down – no sign of Abe. He crossed the street and did the same there and saw someone coming out of a store carrying a bag. He had to run a few blocks to catch up – ignoring lights – but he finally spotted him.

Miller watched as his old friend mounted the steps. A Concierge opened the door for him, tipping his hat.

Miller flashed his badge at the concierge then went inside. The elevator doors were closing and heading up to the seventh floor. He considered taking the steps up, but instead waited for the elevator to come back down again. He entered and hit the button and within moments was on the correct floor where he had four doors to choose from. Which one was Abe's? And what was he doing in an apartment in this area? He cautiously moved from door to door, listening with his ear hard against the door for any sounds inside.

He heard nothing until he reached door number four.

CHAPTER SIXTY

THE ROOM

Inside the room, Abe stood stock still as he tried to catch his breath. Was he losing his mind? For a second, he thought he had spotted Alex Miller out there. No way his old friend could have followed him – he had ditched his phone.

He opened the bag and unboxed his new burner phone and plugged it in to charge. Then he pulled out two bags of candy – Benjamin's favourites. He poured them into a dish which he placed on the night table.

As he looked around the room, he noticed two glasses on the coffee table. So, they were there, or had been there. He realized he was thirsty, he poured himself a cool glass of water.

He drank it down, then poured a second glass and held it against his forehead. It felt good, so he kept it in place as he looked around the room.

Behind him the tap dripped. He recalled being in bed after one of their many sessions with Benjamin sleeping beside him. Even then the tap used to drip drip drip. Having to get out of bed, tighten it. Get back in bed and again, drip drip drip. Under the sink he found a wrench and fixed the problem but now it was back again. It had been a while since they were together.

He sat down on the edge of the bed. "Katie? Benjamin?" No reply. He tried again, lifting the comforter up to look under the bed. "I can hear you breathing." He moved toward the balcony, "Come out, come out, wherever you are."

CHAPTER SIXTY-ONE

WHAT THE?

Wait. Miller asked himself, did Abe say their names out loud? He pushed his ear closer. There it was again, the old man was calling the children, like they were playing a game of hide and seek. Miller scratched his head. The tone Abe was using, was playful and familiar. Like he'd done this kind of thing before.

Inside the room he heard footsteps, followed by the sound of a door opening then closing. He kept his ear pressed against the door, as a toilet flushed, the tap screeched, the door opened, and footsteps made their way across the room where a bed creaked. Moments later Miller heard loud snores. Abe's wife was dead, and he was taking a nap.

CHAPTER SIXTY-TWO

THE DREAM

Abe dreamed he was back at home and he was with El. In one moment, they were flying together across the sky. In another they were spooning together on the bed.

She whispered into his ear, "Abe."

"Abe," Benjamin whispered.

"Benjamin?" he said as rose from the bed. No reply.

Abe walked over to the closet. He recalled Benjamin, years ago when he had first come into their home. He was frightened of everyone and everything and he had found comfort by hiding inside a closet.

"I know you're in there," he said sliding the door open. Sure enough, Benjamin was in there. Way, way back against the wall sitting cross-legged.

Abe felt along the wall, looking for a light switch. There wasn't one.

"Come on out, Benjamin," he coaxed. "I brought you chocolates and candies: your favourites." Still, the boy did not move. Abe retreated to where the burner phone was charging. Nearly halfway. He downloaded the flashlight application. He tried it out and it worked fine. He inched his way into the closet with his phone illuminating the way.

Benjamin was holding something, a raggedy doll. Abe zeroed in with the flashlight. The thing he was holding was no doll: it was Katie.

He moved closer, closer. Reached out and touched the boy's cheek then the girl's – they were both stone cold. He screamed a scream to waken the dead.

CHAPTER SIXTY-THREE

BREAK ON THROUGH TO THE OTHER SIDE

Miller kicked down the door with his booted foot. Now inside, he pulled his gun out of the holster as Abe came out of the closet. Like a zombie, he swayed across the floor then fell first to his knees, then, face down on the floor.

Miller still had his gun pointed on Abe who was sobbing and whimpering like a man who had lost his mind. Miller moved closer, trying to figure out what he was saying. At first, he could not make it out, then he heard, "Dead. Dead. Dead."

He turned toward the closet and as the door was already open stepped inside. It was too dark; he couldn't see a damned thing. He stepped out, employed the tactical flashlight on his weapon and went back inside.

CHAPTER SIXTY-FOUR

BODIES

The flashlight was too strong for such a confined small space. The rays bounced and created dark shadows before they zeroed in on what was there. Two children: Benjamin and Katie.

At first, he thought they were sleeping. He ran the light over their eyes. First the boy, then the girl. He was sure now. He had seen it so many times. The two children looked like the cadavers laid out on the slabs at the morgue.

He touched Katie's face and flinched: it was stone cold. Poor child. Died without knowing she was right about her mother. Benjamin was also cold.

He knew he ought not move them. He ought not disturb their final resting place. And yet, even though he knew better. Even though he realized he would be disturbing the evidence, he still did it.

Miller first had to untangle them. Benjamin's arms were around Katie, like he was trying to protect her. Her head lolled and rested on his shoulder. Her hair, smelling of honey, brushed against his cheek as he set her down on the bed. He returned to the closet, casting a glance at Abe as he went. He was still on the floor, looking ahead like a zombie. Miller picked Benjamin up and depositing him on the bed.

Glancing at Abe, scratching his head, he thought about his own kids. How could this have happened? What did it have to do with El's death? "What happened man?" he said to Abe.

Abe drew himself up onto his knees. He had no strength to pull himself to his feet. His head lolled and his eyes stared at the floor.

Miller shouted, "What in the Sam hell happened here?"

Abe sobbed, then flung himself down onto the rug. He pressed his full face into the carpeting like feeling the rough fabric against his skin was comforting to him.

Miller went closer, so his boots were touching Abe's head. He whispered, "Katie was right – her mother is alive."

"What?" Abe replied.

"It doesn't matter now," Miller said. "She's dead. They're both dead."

This time Abe banged his forehead on the floor.

Miller poured himself a glass of water. He drank it down, but it came right back up again while the tap drip dripped in the background. He thought about taking water to Abe. He didn't.

"Stand up, Abe," Miller demanded. When he was upright, Miller shook his shoulders, "Explain yourself, man."

Abe began to snivel and cry. He crumpled onto his knees.

Miller went to the closet, pulled out a blanket and draped it over Abe's shoulders. He tried not to think of the children, instead focusing on things he needed to do. He needed to call the coroner and get things in motion for an investigation. Why was he hesitating? What was he waiting for? It did not make sense – none of it. The kids were stone cold – like they had been dead for a while – when according to El, they couldn't have been gone long. So, what had happened? Who was responsible? He phoned it in, offering little explanation. "Two deceased children: cause unknown," he said.

As he waited to speak to his commander, he glanced at the two children on the bed. They looked frightened - like they had been frightened to death. He shook his head. People could die from many things, but not from fear.

After he disengaged the call, he went back to Abe. "What in god's name happened here?" He helped Abe to his feet, leading him toward the sink for a glass of water.

Abe took a sip, then said, "I need air!" He strode across the room and threw back the door which led to the balcony.

Miller stood within the arches of the patio door; afraid his old friend might jump.

From somewhere in the room a child sobbed.

Abe and Miller turned toward the bed, knowing full well the sound had not come from there. Both men stood stalk still, with every sense on high alert as they waited to hear the sound again.

"Coroner," a voice outside said after knocking.

"It's open," Miller said as the team, including forensics arrived.

Miller glanced at Abe, who was sitting expressionless. His blue eyes looked even more blue hidden in his ghostly pallor.

"What do we have here?" a member of the forensic team asked.

"Two dead kids," Miller replied.

The team got to work securing evidence.

Miller and Abe stood side by side waiting for the sound: the sound of a whimpering child.

CHAPTER SIXTY-FIVE

THE PAINTING

Abe lifted himself up and moved forward, cocking his head like he'd heard something.

Miller heard nothing. He opened his mouth to say something to Abe, but it was like he was in a trance. He shuffled his feet across the carpet.

Abe fell to his knees sobbing out the words, "I'm sorry, Benjamin. So sorry. All I want is for you to be here. Please." His body fell forward with his head resting on the carpet.

Miller was of two minds. One was to comfort his old friend who was hallucinating. The other was to assist the team – they were nearly ready to put the two children into body bags.

Instead, he did nothing, as Benjamin was zipped into the green bag. He shivered as the second sound of the zipper closing Katie in cut through the silence.

"Stand up," a voice from nowhere commanded.

Abe did so, rising to his feet like a puppet brought to life by a puppeteer.

"Go to the painting," the voice directed.

Abe followed the directions like a zombie, stopping at the Van Gogh print.

"No! No!" he screamed, covering his head with his hands.

Miller moved directly behind him, so he could have a closer look at the reprint. All he saw was a vase of sunflowers– not that he'd expected to see anything else. When Abe started speaking again, Miller moved away.

Abe removed his hands from his face and sobbed, "Why? Why? Why? Tell me why?"

The team carrying the bodies of the children advanced toward the door. One asked, "Who's the old geezer talking to?"

Without answering, Miller waved him away.

A voice rang out. A boy's voice which sounded hollow, like it was coming from inside a tunnel. "You know why."

"Benjamin," Abe said. "I love you."

The team with the body bags stopped. They didn't know the voice they were hearing, was Benjamin's - the boy whose body was in one of the bags they were carrying.

"Put the bags back on the bed," Miller ordered. "Unzip the one with the boy in it – NOW."

The team did as Miller instructed. Benjamin was white, eyes closed. Still dead. Miller stared at the motionless face of the boy, as his voice sounded again.

"You know what you did to me. You know."

"I have loved you. I still love you," Abe replied, reaching out to the empty air.

"Loved who? Who is he talking to, Van Gogh himself?" one of the team members asked.

"Shhh," Miller replied.

"What we did, was love. Because we loved one another," Abe confessed.

Miller shook his head. Was he hearing right? He clenched his fists as he closed the gap between him and his former friend.

Abe looked up at the ceiling, like he thought Benjamin was talking to him from Heaven.

"Why did you have to kill yourself and Katie? Why?"

"I did what I had to do."

"To punish me?"

"Yes, because I know you."

Miller clenched his fists.

"I wouldn't have touched her," Abe sobbed.

"I don't believe you."

Abe remained statuesque in front of the painting with his eyes gazing skyward.

Miller mouthed the words to the team behind him, "I'll take it from here."

They zipped up Benjamin's bag and carried the two children out of the room.

Miller moved so Abe was directly in front of him.

Abe continued looking skyward. Time seemed to stop.

Then a knife thrust out of the painting and in one quick motion slit Abe's throat.

For a few seconds Abe remained in the same position. The only movement was blood gushing from the wound. Then gravity took over, and he dropped to the floor with his head disappearing under the bed covering.

CRASH. The framed Van Gogh sunflower painting dropped to the floor. The glass frontispiece shattered, splintering into a thousand pieces.

Miller called the team back. When they reentered the room, the floor was a bloody mess. "Where's his head?" one asked.

Miller spoke like it was an everyday occurrence. "It's under the bed."

One raised the duvet, the other reached under. They stuffed Abe into the body bag with his eyes wide open. It had happened so fast; he hadn't had time to blink. They zipped up the body bag.

"Don't put the kids anywhere near him," Miller said. Put him in the trunk, or on the roof, anywhere – but not with those kids."

"Sure thing, we'll see to it."

CHAPTER SIXTY-SIX

SGT. MILLER

Miller went out onto the balcony to get a little fresh air. He needed to think it all through because none of it made sense. First there was El's death. Had she known what was going on with her husband and foster child? He did not believe she could have known. Not El.

Benjamin and Katie looked like they'd been frightened to death – but they were dead long before Abe arrived in this place.

As to Abe's abuse of his foster son, it was twisted. Too twisted to think about. He didn't want to think of how many times Abe had been a guest in his own home. Of the times Abe had spent with his own children.

Then there was the supernatural aspect of what happened. Sgt. Miller didn't believe in the supernatural. He'd seen it though and he'd heard the voices. But how was he going to explain it? He'd never be able to in a million years.

The world had gone mad.

Miller returned inside, slamming the balcony doors shut and locking them. A man and a woman were there with a vacuum and a carpet cleaning machine.

The woman asked, "Okay if I start?" to Miller, who nodded. She turned on the vacuum machine and for a few seconds he stood listening to the glass being sucked into the metal container.

"Stop!" he ordered, as he moved across the floor. He bent down and picked up a single sunflower on a piece of glass.

The woman went back to vacuuming again, while Miller held the sunflower up to his eyes.

Then he saw it – movement – inside the sunflower. Paints, chrome yellow, lemon yellow, colours swirling and turning like a kaleidoscope. He felt the carpet shift under him, as he dropped the sunflower then everything went black as he fell to the floor.

CHAPTER SIXTY-SEVEN

KATIE WAKES UP

"Benjamin," Katie said, "I'm not meant to be here." She was on a swing and he was pushing her higher and higher, but not too high.

"Of course, you should be here," Benjamin said.

Children all around them played. A few were in the sandbox. Others were teeter tottering. Many competed in baseball and soccer games. Several played board games like chess, checkers, and marbles.

"You are welcome here," a boy, younger than Benjamin said to Katie.

He wore denim overalls, without a shirt underneath. He had a golden tan which made his blond hair and blue eyes dominant on his athletic face.

"You are very welcome here, my new sister," a little girl, younger than Katie said. Her hair was in ringlets, which bounced when she ran. She looked pretty, in a blue dress with lace around the edges and on her feet were white sandals.

"But I'm not like you," Katie said. "I don't belong here. You heard Sgt. Miller. He said my mommy is alive. She's probably waiting for me at the waterfront. She told me not to move. She'll be worried about me."

Benjamin pushed her higher, "You'll be safe here."

Tumbleweeds blew through the park. The park inside the shattered Van Gogh Sunflowers painting. The place where all the forgotten children lived and played together forever.

For although the glass front shattered in this world, it remained intact in another. Each child's time clock reversed, back.

Back. To the time when they lost their childhood. When they were forced to grow up, too fast.

Inside the painting, the children remained children forever. In the safety of Van Gogh's sunny Sunflowers there was a promise. A promise no child would ever be hurt, abused, frightened, or neglected ever again.

CHAPTER SIXTY-EIGHT

SGT. MILLER

At the morgue, Miller was choosing caskets for El, Katie and Benjamin – and Abe. He would have let the old man go to the deuces into a cardboard box, if he could, but it did not sit right with him. So, he had to choose four caskets for four bodies. Someone had to do it.

Miller hoped to get closure by tending to this task. Still, Katie's missing mother Jennifer Walker played upon his mind. She was out there, somewhere – and her daughter was dead because she had left her alone at the waterfront. Such a tragedy.

Such and loss. All preventable. A parent was meant to protect a child – no matter what.

To put themselves at risk rather than have the child harmed. When did it all go wrong and why didn't he see it?

Miller could not get closure. He could not get piece of mind.

And in his gut, something gnawed away. Eating him from the inside out. He returned to the Julius' home, hoping to find answers. The property was still cordoned off with tape with an officer stationed at the front door.

"Anyone in there?" Miller asked.

"No, Sarge. Think they have pretty much wrapped it up for the day. They've dusted it for prints and taken out anything they wanted to keep for evidence." He looked at his watch. "I was planning to return to the station soon. My shift is nearly over."

"Is someone else coming to watch the place overnight?" Miller asked.

"I don't think so."

"Off you go then," Miller said, "I'll take it from here."

The officer got into his cruiser and drove off. Miller watched him drive away, then entered the house.

Once inside, he let the feeling which was gnawing at his gut lead him to where he needed to go. Down the hall, along the corridor. To Abe's office. He checked the desk: locked. He went into the kitchen and took a knife out of the drawer. He used it to break into the desk. What he was looking for was sitting there, almost like it was waiting for him: Abe's ledger.

Miller flipped through the pages leading up to Christmas, looking for doll orders. There were several orders over the years including photos of the children, their full addresses, and photos of the children with their matching dolls.

There was not one of Katie in the pile though, but he was able to confirm the person who placed the order and had collected the doll had been Mark Wheeler.

He found seven in total orders from over the years. A photo of the child, next to the photo of the doll. Katie's had been the last purchase.

He sat in Abe's chair for a few seconds more, as he flipped through his files. Notable was an application to adopt Benjamin. It said he would also take ownership of the house and the store. Nothing had been finalized, as El hadn't signed it. He grabbed the application along with the ledger and carried them out of the office.

He went into Katie's room. For a second, he could not breathe. Her look-alike doll was on the bed, sitting up, watching him. Waiting for him. If the thing had been breathing, it could not have stunned him more. Unable to move, his senses heightened.

First, a whistling sound. Flapping. Billowing curtains. Reaching out for the doll like fabric tentacles.

He shivered, turned to leave but could not. He wrapped his arms around himself.

"Okay, okay," he said to no one. He scooped up the doll and carried it out of the room and into the kitchen. He looked under the sink for a bag big enough to tuck it into. He didn't have the heart to put it into a green garbage bag – too much like a body bag. Instead, he found a blue see through recycling bag and put the doll in feet first.

He locked up the house, got into his car and drove across town. Arriving at the building, the concierge recognized him, so he didn't have to show his badge. Good thing since he was carrying a doll in a large see-through bag.

"I'll take you up there," Matthew Barry, the Desk Manager said. He led the way into the elevator and on up to the seventh floor.

In the elevator on the way up, Miller asked himself lots of questions, like what he was doing and why, but no answers came.

All he knew for certain was, since he picked up the doll, the feeling which had been eating away at his gut lessened. As he drew nearer to the room, it faded into the background.

Barry turned the key in the lock, and WHAM, a siren screamed – making the Manager feel like his brain would explode. The poor guy clicked every button on the wall – trying to make the violent sound stop. When nothing worked, he covered his ears, and eventually turned and went screaming out of the room.

Miller was affected by the sirens too, but not as much as the Manager had been. He fell onto the bed, using the pillows to muffle the sound and hoped it would stop soon. He closed his eyes and blacked out. When he came to the pillows were on the floor and the room was quiet.

He gulped a little water, then splashed a bit onto his face. He noticed the carpet was new, plusher this time. Then he saw something else: a new Van Gogh Sunflowers painting enclosed in an antique gold frame.

While the tap drip-dripped, he examined the painting. Saw no movement, then remembered the doll. He saw the plastic bag on the floor beside the bed: it was empty.

Scratching his head, he turned and walked toward the door, and as he placed his hand on the doorknob, children's voices serenaded:

Thank you for the flowers,
Thank you for the trees,
Thank you for the waterfalls,
Thank you for the breeze.
We are here together now.
Free from harm and pain
Thank you, Sgt. Miller
For coming back again.

Those words and the tune continued going around and around in his head. For days, weeks, months, years.

EPILOGUE

Miller took his retirement, with one final request in the line of duty. He knocked on Judy Smith's door.

"I'm here to see Gerald," he said.

He followed Judy up the stairs, "Sgt. Miller is here to see you."

She stood in the doorway, while Miller shook Gerald's hand and presented him with a Citizen's Commendation.

"You helped us solve a case," Miller said. "Keep up the excellent work."

"Can I get a photo of the two of you?" Judy asked.

Miller nodded and he and Gerald chatted while she went downstairs and came back up again with her phone in her hand.

"Say cheese," she said.

After a few photos, Miller said his goodbyes and was on his way home. He was hoping for a quiet night with his wife – what he didn't know was, she had a huge surprise retirement party waiting for him.

Acknowledgments

Thank you for reading Everyone's Child which I first wrote the first draft of during National Novel Writing Month way back in 2013.

First draft completed, I did some minor edits then sent it out to some beta readers to see how it could be improved - and if they liked it. Four out of five readers (who were fellow authors) did not like Katie, nor Benjamin and wanted me to rewrite the characters to be more like their own children, etc. I took their away to mull them over while I worked on other projects.

In the end, I decided to stick to my guns. Other authors could write their characters the way they wanted to write them. If we all wrote our characters in the same way, what would be the point? These were my characters and they'd chosen me to tell their stories to/through. I had to tell their stories in the way they wanted them to be heard. In that regard, my characters and myself were in sync.

Which sent me searching for a Developmental Editor and I found an excellent one and for her help and encouragement I will always be grateful.

But Everyone's Child wasn't finished yet. It needed to be read by new beta readers and it was. I asked them questions this time, and in particular I was concerned about bread crumbs. Had I left enough along the way to lead the reader to the shocking conclusion? One out of five readers thought I'd given too much away and asked me to reduce the number of bread crumbs. You might be interested to know that she guessed wrong initially, but by rereading she picked up on more of the hints I'd given.

I'd like to take this opportunity to thank my proof readers, beta readers, editors for their commitment to myself and this project. Your input was valuable - whether I accepted your suggestions or not. For helping me to make Everyone's Child the best it could be. Perhaps Stephen King could have/would have done more. But I'm no Stephen King. I'm an Indie Author, sole employee and founder of Stratford Living Publishing.

Thank you also to family and friends who stood by me through the darkness.

And as always, Happy Reading!

Cathy

ABOUT THE AUTHOR

Multi-award-winning author, Cathy McGough lives and
writes in Oakville,
Ontario, Canada with her husband, son and two cats.
If you'd like to email Cathy,
you can reach her here:
cathy@cathymcgough.com.
Cathy loves to hear from
her readers.

FICTION

Ribby's Secret

The Umbrella and the Wind

Margaret's Revelation

Dandelion Wine (READERS' FAVOURITE BOOK AWARD FINALIST)

Interviews With Legendary Writers From Beyond (2ND PLACE BEST LITERARY REFERENCE 2016 METAMORPH PUBLISHING)

Plus Size Goddess

NON-FICTION

103 Fundraising Ideas For Parent Volunteers With Schools and Teams (3RD PLACE BEST REFERENCE 2016 METAMORPH PUBLISHING)

Manufactured by Amazon.ca
Bolton, ON

26533759R00127